DRAG-STRIP
RACER

Books by Matt Christopher

Sports Stories

The Lucky Baseball Bat
Baseball Pals
Basketball Sparkplug
Little Lefty
Touchdown for Tommy
Break for the Basket
Baseball Flyhawk
Catcher with a Glass Arm
The Counterfeit Tackle
Miracle at the Plate
The Year Mom Won the
  Pennant
The Basket Counts
Catch That Pass!
Shortstop from Tokyo
Jackrabbit Goalie
The Fox Steals Home
Johnny Long Legs
Look Who's Playing First Base
Tough to Tackle
The Kid Who Only Hit Homers
Face-Off
Mystery Coach
Ice Magic
No Arm in Left Field

Jinx Glove
Front Court Hex
The Team That Stopped Moving
Glue Fingers
The Pigeon with the Tennis
  Elbow
The Submarine Pitch
Power Play
Football Fugitive
Johnny No Hit
Soccer Halfback
Diamond Champs
Dirt Bike Racer
The Twenty-One-Mile Swim
The Dog That Stole Football
  Plays
Run, Billy, Run
Wild Pitch
Tight End
Drag-Strip Racer

Animal Stories

Desperate Search
Stranded
Earthquake
Devil Pony

DRAG=STRIP RACER

MATT CHRISTOPHER

LITTLE, BROWN AND COMPANY
BOSTON   **TORONTO**

F
Chr

FIRST EDITION

Library of Congress Cataloging in Publication Data

Christopher, Matt.
  Drag-strip racer.

  Summary: When he inherits a racing car, sixteen-year-
old Ken determines to become a drag racer.
  [1. Drag racing—Fiction] I. Title.
PZ7.C4577Dr   [Fic]   81-19378
ISBN 0-316-13904-1   AACR2

BP

Published simultaneously in Canada
by Little, Brown & Company (Canada) Limited

PRINTED IN THE UNITED STATES OF AMERICA

12135

To Carl, Bruce, and Bradley

DRAG-STRIP RACER

ONE

THE EARLY MORNING silence was heavy in the Ford pickup as it traveled at a steady forty-five-mile-per-hour clip on Route 60 to Candlewyck Speedway. The stillness was broken only by the rhythmic sound of the motor and the *thump-thump* of the tires crossing the tar-patched stripes on the highway.

Behind the wheel, sixteen-year-old Ken Oberlin glanced at his sister, Janet, sitting beside him. "Excited?"

"Yes."

"I'm glad," he said. "You and Lori are the only ones on my side. Neither Mom or Dad is keen about my drag racing. But Uncle Louis left Li'l Red to me, so what am I supposed to do? Toss her on a junk pile?"

Janet looked at him, her coffee-brown eyes

shining. "Well, they *did* let you drive it in autocrosses," she said. At fourteen she had taken an interest in cars herself, although she still had two years to go before she could get a driver's license.

"Yes, and I'm glad I did," he told her. "But autocrosses are mainly for precision and skill. I think I learned a lot, but what I'm interested in now is speed. Boy, I wish Uncle Louis hadn't died. I mean, if he was just around to give me a little advice now and then."

Uncle Louis was his father's brother, a dragstrip freak from his teenage years to the day he passed away of a heart attack at age fifty-nine.

Ken thought back to the times his uncle had taken him for rides in Li'l Red, times he'd seen her blazing down the 1320-foot asphalt strip to more victories than he could remember. They were glorious memories.

"What does Dana think about it?" Janet asked.

"I don't care what he thinks," Ken said stiffly. "He's got his motorcycle, I've got my car."

He'd never forget the cold stare his brother had given him when the words of Uncle Louis's will were read by his attorney: *I bequeath my racer, Li'l Red, to my nephew Kenneth, who I hope will enjoy racing it with all the pleasure that it has given me.*

4

Sometimes he wondered if Dana was really a member of their family. The guy had left school a month before he was supposed to graduate, telling the family he was positive he wouldn't pass the final exams anyway. Now he worked part time at Nick Evans's pool parlor, and from the money he earned had managed to buy himself a Kawasaki motorcycle.

"How much farther do we have to go?" Janet asked, as she looked down the gleaming white road. It was flanked on either side by brush and pasture fields. A couple of dozen cattle grazed monotonously.

"About two, maybe three miles," Ken said.

Minutes later they could see the towering sign in the distance: Candlewyck Speedway. Soon Ken changed to the right-turn-only lane, reached the intersection, and turned through an open gate. He paused at the ticket office, showed his pre-entry card to a red-haired woman working there, drove through another gate, and turned left toward the technical inspection station.

He showed the card again to one of three guys in white coveralls with "Inspector" labels sewn on the left sides of their chests. Then he got out of the pickup, unlocked the chain securing the racer, lowered the ramp, and drove the red Chevy off the trailer and onto a weighing scale. He emerged from it to permit the men to continue their inspection of the car's height, engine size, tires, and carburetor. The men made check marks on their tablets, then — about fifteen minutes later — stepped back and told Ken he was set to run. Over a walkie-talkie one of the men informed the timing tower that "a red 1975 Chevy owned and driven by Ken Oberlin has passed inspection and is coming in for its trial runs."

"Is it necessary to go through this full inspection every day?" Ken asked the man.

"No. There'll be just a quick check once a week after this, unless you don't show up for two or three weeks," the tech man told him, smiling.

"Thanks."

Ken drove the Chevy back on the trailer, then drove the trailer to the pit stop, a long vacant lot facing the track, and saw an ambulance along with three other trucks and trailers there. The owners of the trucks and trailers were on the lanes, trial-running their cars.

Ken felt a rush of excitement as he parked, shut off the engine, and watched the trial runs. The three cars present were an orange Omni, a yellow Vega, and a blue Camaro, each emblazoned on the side with the driver's name and the commercial outfit sponsoring him. Having a commercial company behind you wasn't necessary, but it helped when it came to paying for supplies and repairs. Ken, aware of the tightness of money in his household, hoped to find a sponsor soon.

"You going to sit here all day?" Janet said suddenly, glancing casually at him.

Ken looked at her and smiled. He got out, walked back to the trailer, and lowered the ramp again to drive Li'l Red off.

Soon he was back inside the two-door Chevy that was powered by a 1970, 396-horsepower big block engine Uncle Louis had installed himself. He started the car, backed it up, and let it idle while he climbed out to take his firesuit, helmet, and gloves from a duffel bag and put them on.

He glanced up at the top windows of the dome-shaped tower building and thought he saw one of the track co-owners — either Buck Morrison or Jay Wells — looking out at him.

A moment later a voice boomed over a loudspeaker: "Ken Oberlin, drive around the timing tower and get ready to run against the Camaro. Take number one lane, please. You have three trial runs. Your best time will be used to determine your run for this afternoon's Eliminator contest."

7

Ken acknowledged the order by raising a hand; then he drove around the tower toward lane one and stopped as a crewman standing on the lanes behind the two cars that were ready to run raised his hand. A moment later the blue Camaro drove up and stopped beside him, ready to get on lane two.

Ken glanced at the driver — Bill Robbins, according to the name blazing in white across the door. Robbins turned to him and raised a thumb, and Ken acknowledged the sign by raising his.

He knew very few drivers personally. He had trial-run his car only twice before to get the feel of its power and performance. This morning was the first time he was going to trial-run it to qualify for drag racing. It was going to be the Big Event for him, the start of something great. Maybe.

Yeah, maybe, he told himself. Even Uncle Louis had never won the Winternationals, the Gatornationals, or any other national event. But he'd been close to it a dozen times. And he'd made a name for himself in the world of Pro Stock racing.

They got the signal to move ahead. Ken moved the gear lever, jammed his foot on the gas pedal, and felt the slicks take a solid grip of the rosin-topped asphalt as the car shot forward. Then he slammed on the brakes, paused a moment, and repeated the procedure. Satisfied that the tires were doing their job, he drove up to the staging lane and braked when the top yellow light of the "Christmas tree," about twenty feet down the course, flashed on.

It was hot inside the car. Sweat dripped from his forehead into his eyes, blurring his vision. He lifted the plastic shield of his helmet and wiped his eyes with the tip of his gloved finger, then waited for the staged lights of the Christmas tree to be activated.

Suddenly they were, and he glued his attention on them; every muscle in his body responded with tension as, one by one, the amber lights turned on. Only two and a half seconds elapsed from the time the lights turned on till the green starting light activated. Take off too soon and a red light flashed, indicating a foul start and an automatic loss. Take off too late and you might as well forget it. Most races were won or lost at the starting line, so it paid to concentrate one hundred percent on the lights.

There! The last amber light went on, then the green — and Ken jammed on the gas pedal. He felt his body thrust back against the seat as the car sprang forward, the front end tilting up on its frame for a second or two, then settling back down. All of her 396 horsepower responded as a unit. Ken's hand on the five-speed stick shift was white-knuckled and trembled under the severe strain of the screaming transmission. He braced his teeth as he felt his skin draw back against his jaw. He shifted into the next gear, the 4¾-inch travel from one gear to the next feeling liquid smooth.

The car blazed down the track, engine roaring. The best Ken had done so far in Li'l Red was 12.08 at 112.67 miles per hour. He was sure the car could do better. She had the power harnessed inside that metal body. Uncle Louis had learned to use it to her upper limits. I should, too, Ken told himself.

He reached the end of the quarter-mile run and stepped on the brakes. The car slowed briefly, then something seemed to spring loose and the car continued its swift speed down the lane.

Stunned and gripped with fear, Ken kept pumping the brake pedal. But the brakes still didn't respond. Oh, no, he thought, what happened to the brakes?

Then he felt the car pull to the right. It was traveling so fast he was off the lane before he knew it. He had a blurred glimpse of the Camaro beside him, and, in an effort to avoid a collision with it, he swung the wheel to the left. The momentum of the car's speed carried him across the lane toward the guardrail. He turned the wheel to the right to avoid hitting it, but struck it with the side of his left front fender. At the same time he felt a jarring pain in his left foot, which he had braced against the floorboard.

He veered back onto the asphalt and headed toward the metal fence in the distance, shoving the shift lever into lower speeds now to slow the car down. Some fifty feet from the fence he made a U-turn and brought the vehicle to a stop, nose pointing toward the pit stops.

He yanked off his helmet, gripped the wheel, and shut his eyes in angry despair.

"What happened?" he cried aloud. "What could have happened?"

He felt the pain in his left ankle again, and wondered if it were sprained or broken. He probably would have to have it x-rayed to make sure. What lousy luck.

He heard a siren screaming in the distance, drawing nearer by the second.

He unbuckled his seat belt, opened the door, and stumbled out of the car. He saw the blue Camaro pull up on the other side of him. Then

Bill Robbins piled out of it and came running forward.

"You okay?" Robbins asked worriedly.

"I'm not sure," Ken said, and looked at his left foot. "My foot jammed against the floorboard when I hit the guardrail. I might have sprained or broken it. I don't know."

"Did you lose control?" Robbins wanted to know.

"The brakes gave."

The ambulance arrived and pulled up beside them. Two paramedics jumped out of it and hurried toward him.

"You okay?" asked the shorter of the two, a stout, reddish-haired guy about twenty-five.

"Okay except for my left foot," Ken answered.

"Lie down," the medic advised. Both he and his partner got on either side of Ken and helped ease him to the ground.

Ken saw a figure racing across the field toward them, hair flying. Janet's eyes were wide with panic as she came running up to him. She stopped and stared down at him as he lay there. A medic had removed Ken's shoe and was examining his injured foot.

Ken felt the gentle, probing fingers. Then they

found a tender spot that flared with hot-iron pain as the medic pressed his thumb against it.

"I'm afraid you've got a fracture, my friend," the medic said. "Hold still. I'll get a stretcher and take you to the hospital."

Janet gazed at the medic as he rose to his feet and started toward the ambulance. "Can I go with him?" she asked. "He's my brother."

"You sure can," he said.

TWO

THE GARAGE DOOR was open and the car was gone. So was Li'l Red. It had been parked under the towering oak next to the garage.

Dana rubbed the dark fuzz on his chin as he remembered that today, Saturday, was a big day for his kid brother. He was going to trial-run the Chevy for this afternoon's Eliminator contest. Well, good luck, old buddy, he thought, as he climbed off his motorcycle.

He yanked off his black helmet, hung it over a handlebar, and rubbed his dark hair vigorously with his hands. Then he combed it back with his fingers and headed for the house, a half-smoked cigarette dangling from his mouth. Just before he reached the front porch he took a deep drag from it, inhaled the smoke into his lungs, then dropped it and squashed it with the heel of his right boot.

His taut, tall frame moved with easy grace as he stepped up to the door and turned the knob. The door was locked.

He knocked, but there was no answer.

"They must've all gone to watch their favorite son do his thing," Dana muttered out loud.

Dana reached for the ring of keys he kept on his wide belt, selected one, and unlocked the door.

He went in, closed the door behind him, plunked his long, angular frame down on an armchair, and yanked off his boots. Then he stretched out his feet, wiggled his toes, and laughed.

"So Ken thinks he's going to make out like good old Uncle Louis, does he?" he said, again voicing his thoughts out loud. "Bull. He'll never be able to carry a candle to that old-timer."

Anyway, he thought with some bitterness, that racer should have been left to him. Ken was no hot-rodder. He was at home with books, not a racing car. He had sat on a motorcycle only once in his life and Dana remembered he had to coax him to get on it then. Why leave a racer to a sixteen-year-old kid when he was afraid to ride pillion on a bike?

Why? Because Ken's the good boy of the

family, that's why, Dana answered his own question. Tell him to do something and he'll jump to it like a puppet on a string.

"Well," he said aloud, "not me. I'm eighteen and I'm going to live my own life. I am what I am, and I'm not going to change it — for Mom, or Dad, or Ken, or anybody else."

He glanced at his wristwatch. Ten after twelve. Well, he'd better make himself a sandwich and get back to work before twelve-thirty, he thought. He was doing a job for Nick Evans — painting the walls of his pool parlor — and Nick didn't like to have his help late. Even part-time help.

He slid off the armchair, went into the kitchen, and headed toward the refrigerator. He saw a note taped to the door and leaned over to read it.

Dana,

We're at the hospital. Ken's foot was fractured in an accident.

I've made a couple of sandwiches for you.

If you can come to see your brother, please do.

Mother

He picked up the note, read it again, then wadded it up into a ball. How do you like that? he thought. The first day of his race and Ken had to go and fracture his foot. That proved that he was no racer. He should stick to his books, or that wood sculpturing hobby he had recently started.

Dana tossed the wadded paper into the garbage container, opened the refrigerator door, and hauled out the two bagged sandwiches along with a can of beer. He thought of going to the hospital to see Ken, but wasn't particularly interested. A fractured foot was no big deal. Ken was lucky he hadn't broken his neck.

He ate the sandwiches and reconsidered. His parents would want him to see Ken, so he decided he would. The hospital was out of his way, but he didn't have to stay there for more than a few minutes. No reason why he couldn't get back to Nick's in time.

He finished the beer, tossed the empty can and bags into the garbage container, locked the house, and biked to the hospital. He found out from the receptionist that Ken was in the emergency ward, and went to it. He didn't hurry. His heels clicked on the tiled floor like a slow-running clock.

The whole family was there — his mother, father, Janet, and ten-year-old Lori. The moment he stepped into the room they turned to him simultaneously, looking as if they were surprised to see him.

Dana noticed, as he had before, that at thirty-nine his father looked ten years older, very gaunt from his serious diabetic condition, but sun-browned from his regular stint in the garden he loved so much. His mother, by comparison, was almost as fit as she had been as a young woman.

They exchanged greetings, then he stepped up to the bed where Ken was lying, his left leg in a plaster cast.

"That's a heck of a way to learn that racing is a man's sport," Dana quipped. They shook hands. "What happened?"

Ken explained. "And don't tell me I can't race it," he added firmly. "What happened to the brakes could've happened to any car."

Dana shrugged. "Right."

"Dana, I think you should check over those brakes for him," his father cut in.

Dana looked at him. "Why?"

"Ken thinks they might've been tampered with."

Dana laughed. "Tampered with? Who'd tamper with the brakes on that car, anyway?"

"Hooligans," snapped his father. "Doing it for kicks. Anyway, Ken says he checked the car out thoroughly and hadn't found anything wrong. I would appreciate it if you'd do it."

I wonder if he'd be that concerned about me, Dana thought. Ever since he could remember, both his mother and father seemed more worried about what happened to Ken than they ever did about him.

"I'm a motorcycle man, Dad," he said. "What I know about cars you can stick into a valve cap."

"Then ask that friend of yours. Taggart," his father suggested.

"Scott Taggart?"

"Yes. He races cars, too, and he fixes them. He should be able to find out if the brakes were tampered with or not."

Dana rubbed his chin thoughtfully. Scott Taggart raced a small block Chevy II but had never managed to come out better than third runner-up in the two years that he competed. Along with the Chevy, he owned a Honda motorcycle, and what he knew about both kinds of vehicles could keep him in a good, steady-paying mechanic's job for a long time. He just didn't seem to like steady jobs.

Dana shrugged. "Okay, Pops. Whatever you say," he said.

"Dana — please," said his mother, looking hurt at the way he had addressed his father.

Dana inhaled, then shook his head and clamped his teeth as he exhaled. "Sorry. Okay, *Dad*." He turned back to his brother and forced a weak grin. "Don't run off and do something crazy, okay?" Then he stepped toward his mother, gave her a peck on the cheek, smiled at his sisters, and headed for the door, the heels of his boots clicking sharply on the vinyl-covered floor.

The cold voice of his father stopped him. "Dana."

Dana paused, turned, and faced him. His father's bad eye, the left one, and the good eye fixed firmly on him.

"Yeah?"

"The garage man said he'd have a tow truck haul the car to the house at about two."

"I'm through work at three," Dana told him.

His father nodded.

Dana turned away and walked out. In the hall he took another deep breath and shook his head. He and his father hadn't gotten along since Dana's elementary-school days. It seemed that there wasn't a thing he did that was right, and, through all the years that he was growing up, the situation hadn't changed. Sometimes he thought it was getting worse.

He got back to the pool parlor, secretly hoping that Nick wouldn't see him coming in. But the suave, dark-complected owner of the only pool hall in the small town of Wade, Florida, was sitting behind the cash register in a close conversation with a blond.

"Hi, Nick," Dana greeted him as he headed for the hall where he'd left the paint can and brush. Behind him he could hear the solid crack of cue balls breaking, then the quieter sounds of balls striking one another.

Nick nodded to him. A few seconds later Dana heard footsteps behind him. He turned and saw that it was Nick, smoke curling up past his eyes from the cigarette he held between his lips.

"You're late," Nick said. He glanced at his watch. "Eight minutes late."

Dana felt a tightening in his stomach. "Ken got in an accident. I rode to the hospital to see him."

"What happened?"

"He fractured his foot. He was running some passes with his racer this morning."

"Too bad."

"He'll be okay."

Dana bent over, picked up the screwdriver lying on the covered paint can, and began prying off the lid. He wished Nick would leave. The guy made him nervous.

He got the lid off, picked up the stirring paddle, and began stirring the paint. He went a little too fast and spilled some of it over the edge of the can and onto the paper the can was sitting on. Hands unsteady, he picked up the brush and wiped it off.

"Take it easy," Nick cautioned. "That stuff's expensive."

"Sorry."

"See you around."

"Right."

He watched Nick turn and leave, the tip of the cigarette glowing red as Nick inhaled on it. Dana suppressed a curse. The last thing he wanted was to let Nick think he could scare him.

He worked ten minutes overtime to make up for arriving late at noon, then telephoned Scott Taggart from a pay telephone a block away from the pool parlor. He explained about the accident and Ken's wish to have the brakes on his racer checked.

"Why does he want them checked?" Taggart wanted to know.

"He thinks they might've been tampered with. Can you be there in half an hour?"

"Make it an hour. Have you got a hydraulic jack?"

"Yes."

"Okay. See you."

The family was all at home when Dana got

there. Ken was resting on the sofa in the living room.

"I've called Scott Taggart," he told Ken. "He'll be here in about an hour."

"Good," his father said.

It was almost four-thirty when Scott drove up on his black, red-trimmed Honda. From the living-room window, Dana watched him park next to the trailer on which the little red racer had been secured again. Then he walked out to meet him, trailed by Ken, who managed awkwardly on a pair of crutches, his cast-encased leg hovering slightly above the ground. The girls, Janet and Lori, were on either side of him, as if watching out for him should he miss a step and lose his balance.

Greetings were exchanged as Scott unsnapped his helmet and hung it over a handlebar of his motorcycle. Slim, brown-haired, and beady-eyed, he had acquired the nickname "Rat" from the racing establishment.

He and Dana lowered the ramp. Then Dana unlocked the chain and they pushed the car off the trailer. Dana noticed the crumpled left front fender. The fat repair bill his brother faced came immediately to his mind. Well, that was Ken's worry. He had to expect things like this to happen.

He went and got the hydraulic jack from the two-car garage, jacked up the front end of the car, and Scott began to examine the brakes.

Dana, Ken, and the girls watched him with avid interest. Dana expected that his father was watching from a living-room window, too, although he didn't turn around to see.

Within minutes Scott came up with a discovery.

"The master cylinder's shot," he said.

Dana saw Ken's eyes cloud over with doubt. "How can it be?" he said. "There was no leak."

"That's because the cylinder's all rusted inside and the plunger's worn out," Taggart explained. "The minute you hit the pedal that last time, the plunger dropped out and you had no brakes."

Ken nodded. "Okay, Scott. Thanks. What do I owe you?"

"Nothing. Forget it."

Dana glanced at his brother, and for just a moment he wondered if Ken might have suspected him of tampering with the brakes. Ken knew that Dana would have liked to have the little red Chevy for himself, and it might be possible that he thought Dana might pull a malicious trick.

But I couldn't pull a dirty trick like that, Dana thought. Never.

THREE

I THINK you'd better give it up before something else happens. Something much worse than a fractured foot," said Ken's father.

The older man sat in the chair by the window, rocking back and forth with his hands clasped on his lap. The sunlight pouring in the window surrounded his face with a glow and hid the lines that creased it.

"Please don't tell me to quit, Dad," Ken said. "Accidents can happen no matter what I do. Once I get the master cylinder fixed on Li'l Red I'll make sure that she's in tip-top shape every time I get on a racetrack. I promise."

For a few moments his father rocked harder on the chair, his hands clenching and unclenching.

"Sure, sure. I might as well talk to that wall there," he said.

"Well, Uncle Louis *did* will him that car,"

Ken's mother broke in. She was sitting on the sofa, perusing a magazine on organic gardening. "And Ken really doesn't have any other interests."

Ken was startled by her remark. "That's not true, Mom," he said. "Isn't basketball an interest? And what about those computers? And sculpting models out of tree branches?"

"Yes, but how long did those hobbies last?"

"I'm still sculpting."

"All right, but how often?"

"Once a week — at least."

"Or less," she said.

It was two years ago that he had toyed around with computers. He had made one from kits, but his interest in it had flagged and he began sculpting models out of tree branches. Birds, mainly, because he found them the easiest to do. He didn't know of any kids who sculpted from tree branches. That was what he liked, doing something that wasn't easy and popular. That's why he enjoyed drag racing. There was something different about sitting behind the wheel of a stock car and giving it all it had down a quarter-of-a-mile stretch. Something alive and vibrant.

"Well, you can't race again until your foot heals and the brakes are fixed," his father said. "From what I see that's going to be a long time."

Ken looked down at his cast-covered leg, "Not as long as you think, Dad," he said assuredly.

His father looked at him. His mouth opened and a nerve twitched at the side of his neck.

But he said nothing, as if what he'd say might not make any difference anyway.

Ken knew it wouldn't be easy. He'd have to forgo his summer job at Cowosocki Camp until he was able to maneuver around better. But he'd get that fender straightened and the master cylinder fixed as soon as possible and pay for them out of his savings. He had no problem in that department — yet.

It wasn't till the following Wednesday that he called up Dusty Hill, owner of an automotive parts store that catered to the racing car trade. Dusty also owned the garage next to his shop and was vain enough to tell his customers that the best mechanic in town — not *one* of the best, but *the* best — was right there in his shop. His name was Rooster Falls.

Dusty had another sideline — he sponsored drivers in drag races, a point that Ken had considered before he made the call.

"Hi, Mr. Hill," he said, getting the owner on the line after the third ring. "This is Ken Oberlin. I don't know if you know me, but — "

"Yes, I know you. You're Lou Oberlin's nephew," Dusty interrupted. "I heard you had some trouble at the trial runs last Saturday."

He had a voice that seemed to come from the bottom of a well. And he talked slowly, as if measuring each word before uttering it.

"Right," Ken said. "The master cylinder went bad and I — well, I came out of it with a fractured foot."

"You were lucky. What can I do for you?"

"I'd like to get the brakes fixed and the front left fender straightened."

"Okay, but it won't be for another week or two," Dusty answered promptly. "I've only got one mechanic and he's up to his back pockets with work. Anyway," he added, chuckling, "you're in no hurry, are you? You can wait another month. Maybe two."

"No, Mr. Hill," Ken said. "I'd like to get the car fixed as soon as possible. It's my left leg in a cast, so I can still drive."

There was a pause. Finally Dusty's slow voice came back over the wire. "Okay, Ken. I'll get my book. Hold on a second."

In half a minute Dusty was back on the phone, an appointment was made, and Ken hung up. He felt the sudden grip of impatience because he knew that the ten days he'd have to wait for his car to get fixed would seem like an eternity.

He heard the back door open and close, and pretty soon saw his father come in and sit down on a chair in the kitchen. He started to take off his shoes, a wide patch of sweat gluing his gray shirt to his back.

He didn't see Ken till he'd kicked off the shoes and straightened up in his chair. Tiny rivers of perspiration trickled slowly down the thin lines of his face, but he didn't seem to notice.

"I've just made an appointment to get my car fixed, Dad," Ken said.

"Oh?" His father's eyebrows arched. "You think you'll be able to race Li'l Red again, even with that cast on your leg?"

Ken smiled. "The cast is on my left leg, Dad," he pointed out, "not on my gas foot."

Less than two weeks later, on a Friday, Ken drove the pickup and trailer to Dusty Hill's garage to bring back the Chevy racer. Rooster drove it up the ramp and onto the trailer, then got out and stood on the ground, looking at it admiringly.

"A real pussycat," he said, wiping his hands on a grease cloth. He was a small man in his forties, with thick black hair and a toothbrush mustache. "Dusty told me it was your uncle's."

"Yes," Ken said. "He wanted me to have it after he died."

Rooster nodded. He and Ken were standing at the side of the car, its sheen so bright that their reflections mirrored clearly back at them. Ken thought the job Rooster had done on the fender was excellent and was going to voice his appreciation, when the mechanic interrupted. "Louis Oberlin. I knew him well. He was good, but he never *could* make the top, could he?" He turned to Ken and his mild, gray eyes sparkled. "Maybe you will."

Ken smiled. "You never know."

"That's right. You never know."

Ken paid Dusty Hill by check, then drove away with the car. He began to ponder his next move and whistled as he did so. He couldn't wait to get home to make another phone call, this one to Buck Morrison, co-owner of Candlewyck Speedway.

The earliest he could use the track was on Monday, Morrison told him. The morning trial runs and the afternoon races on Saturday and Sunday tied up the weekend.

Ken rushed through breakfast on Monday

morning, then drove the pickup, with Li'l Red on the trailer, to the track. Janet begged to go along with him, so he took her. He had a feeling that when she came of age she might try racing, too. She showed a lot of interest in it.

An overcast sky promised rain by the time he swung through the open gate and he wished it would hold off till he got in a few passes. He drove up near the timing tower where Buck Morrison's red pickup was parked. Buck and his partner, Jay Wells, were probably up there in their office, getting the weekend's racing results compiled for the newspapers or preparing for next weekend's races.

Ken wished he could have the Christmas tree out there on the track. Getting used to starting with it despite his cast would be good practice. But he knew that neither Buck nor Jay would drag it out of the building and set it up for him or anybody else.

He unloaded the Chevy and drove it to the staging lanes. It purred like a cat, and the brakes responded quickly and smoothly to the slightest pressure.

He got out, put on his firesuit, gloves, and helmet, and got back into the car. He buckled his seat belt, then looked at Janet and smiled.

She raised two fingers, said, "Good luck," and backed away from the track. A rising wind stirred her hair.

Ken drove the Chevy up near the number one staging lane, where he sat for a moment while he listened to the purring engine and looked down the long ribbon of asphalt ahead of him. He tried to visualize a car on the lane next to his, engine buzzing like a chain saw, its driver bent on getting that all-important start.

He set his cast-laden leg in place, and settled his right foot on the gas pedal. For a second he glanced at the ash-gray sky. No rain yet, but it looked threatening.

He jammed on the gas pedal a couple of times, and each time the Chevy bolted forward a few feet, its rear tires getting a good bite of the rosin-blackened surface.

Then he was in about the spot where he would be if the Christmas tree were set up. He paused a minute, took a few deep breaths, and got ready.

One . . . two . . . three! He hit the gas pedal and the car took off. Its front end leaped, wheels almost leaving the asphalt, yielding all power to the wide-tired, spinning rear wheels. The front tires were regulars and a little used. It wasn't necessary that they be the best, anyway. The demand for the all-out zip and power came mainly from those slick, giant babies in back.

Then the front end settled down and Ken felt the brief impact and the jar of the steering wheel. The car swerved to the left just a little and he righted it gently. Then he glanced at the speedometer and saw the needle quivering at the 104-mile-per-hour mark. How many seconds was that? his mind quickly asked. Thirteen? Fourteen? In that neighborhood, he assumed.

He touched the brakes and smiled as he felt them take hold. He pressed harder, and the car slowed up and then stopped on a dime as he gave the brake pedal a final thrust. All this time he had scarcely thought of the cast on his other leg.

"Good ol' Rooster," he said aloud, smacking the steering wheel with affection. "Well, now for another shot."

He drove back to the number one staging lane, shouting, "How does she look?" to Janet as he rolled slowly past her.

"Just great!" she cried.

He ran the car again and again, each time feeling that he had done better than the time before. It was nearly noon when he decided that he and the Chevy had had enough. The overcast sky had been slightly burned away by the sun, which glowed like a dim yellow ball behind fragments of clouds that flowed in front of it. It hadn't rained and it wasn't likely to.

They returned home and, because Mrs. Oberlin was working and would not be home till shortly after four o'clock, Janet fixed lunch for Ken, Lori, their father, and Dana, who had pulled into the driveway only seconds after Ken.

"Well, had her on the track?" he asked.

"Yes."

"How'd she do?"

"Just fine."

"You didn't have trouble with that bad leg?"

"Not a bit."

Over lunch he explained what he'd like to do. He'd like to race Li'l Red as soon as possible and he was going to ask Dusty Hill to sponsor him.

"Why Dusty?" Dana wanted to know.

"Because he can afford it," Ken said. "He's got a parts store and a garage. And, as far as I know, he hasn't sponsored a driver in a race this year yet."

He looked at the faces around the table for a reaction. His father's eyes came up from beneath tired lids and fastened wearily on him.

"I'm not too crazy about your racing, you

34

know that," his father said. "And neither is your mother."

"It's safe, Dad, if that's what you're worried about," Ken tried to assure him. "It's not like the oval races, or the Indy 500."

"Safe? Your brakes gave once, didn't they?" his father reminded him, a dark glint in his eyes. "What makes you so sure something else won't happen the next time? Or the next?"

"There's some risk, sure, Dad," Ken replied quietly. "But anything that's worth shooting for is risky."

He loved his father very much, but there was that bit of overcoddling that he couldn't stand. His father still treated him as though he were a little kid.

Ken knew it stemmed from his earlier years — before he had reached his teens — when he was so shy he played mainly by himself, or with his sisters. He and Dana had seldom played together Dana was much more outgoing than he, and had a lot of friends in the neighborhood with whom he'd rather play.

He glanced at his sisters now and smiled as he saw reassurance on their young faces. They were both for him one hundred percent.

"What do you think, Dana?" he asked his older brother. "You for me or against me?"

At one time he didn't care what Dana thought. He was sure, ever since the will had been read, that his brother resented Uncle Louis's willing the car to him. Nonetheless, Ken wanted his brother's approval.

"I'm for you, brother," Dana answered, a cynical smile on his lips. "After all, what else in this world do you really care to do, anyway?"

Ken prickled, but kept his temper. "Maybe lots more than you think, Dana," he said, and wished he had kept his mouth shut.

Two days later he drove the pickup to "Hill's Automotive Parts," Dusty's store in the Wade Mall. He arrived early, hoping to get there before the customers started to come in, and found the owner in less than a cheerful mood near the rear of the store. Dusty was shoving some of the larger parts on the floor from one place to another, doing it angrily, as if it were a job he detested.

A bell over the door had clanged as Ken entered, but Dusty either hadn't heard it or was deliberately ignoring it.

Ken walked across the floor, skirting a display of clutches and brake shoes, and paused a short distance away from the store owner.

"Be with you in a minute," Dusty said, continuing with his work without glancing up.

"That's okay, Mr. Hill," Ken said. He steadied himself on the crutches, letting the cast-covered leg rest on the floor.

Dusty stopped working then and looked up at him. Sweat glistened on his face. "Oh, hi, Ken," he said. "Didn't know it was you. How you doing?"

"Okay."

Dusty bent over and started moving parts around again. Ken watched him, suddenly realizing that something was different about the place. It wasn't the change Dusty was making, either. It was something else.

In a moment he realized what it was. The big 350-turbo engine that had been sitting near the center of the floor was missing.

"Did you sell that engine, Mr. Hill?" Ken asked.

"Wish I had, kid," Dusty said grimly. He straightened up, took a handkerchief out of his back pocket, and wiped the sweat off his forehead. In his mid-forties, his hair was still dark, but receding. "Some rot-bellied devil broke in here last night or early this morning and stole it. That's well over a thousand bucks, you know that?"

FOUR

NOTHING ELSE was taken, Dusty told Ken. Just the engine.

Ken wondered whether to tell Dusty now what he had come here for. He felt he should wait.

"You're pretty busy, Mr. Hill," he said. "I'll be back later." He headed for the door.

"Wait a minute. Can I do something for you?"

Ken paused and turned. His eyes focused on Dusty's. His heart hammered. "Well, I was going to ask you if — if you'd like to sponsor me in my races."

Dusty frowned, and his eyes lowered to Ken's cast-encased leg. "You expect to race with a cast on that leg?"

"No problem. I did about ten passes on Monday. Had no trouble at all."

38

Dusty stared at him. Then he took a deep breath and started to look about him as if for another box of parts to move.

"Ken, I feel for you, believe me," he said. "But you're pretty young, you know. You're just getting your feet wet. Drag racing ain't for everybody."

Ken felt as if a needle had been stuck into his skin. "It *is* for me," he said. "I can drive, Mr. Hill. I can drive better than you think."

Dusty moved a box, straightened up, and shrugged. "Okay, maybe you can," he admitted. "But you're too late, anyway. I've already signed up with a driver. I guess I should have told you that in the first place."

Ken froze. He eyed the older man steadily for a few seconds before he could swallow his disappointment.

"Mind telling me who?" he finally asked.

"Scott Taggart. I guess you know him."

Ken nodded. "Yes, I know him. When did you sign up with him?"

Dusty thought a minute. "Two days ago," he said.

Ken nodded again. He stood around awhile longer, then turned and headed for the door. "Sorry I bothered you, Mr. Hill."

"No bother, Ken," Dusty's voice trailed after him.

He opened the door and walked out, squinting against the morning sun. He kept his head down as he hobbled across the sidewalk, stepped off the curb, and started toward his pickup parked in the lot.

Anger and hurt set in his eyes as he thought of what Dusty had said. *"You're just getting your feet wet. Drag racing ain't for everybody."*

But Dusty's sponsoring Scott "Rat" Taggart was the last straw. Taggart had not acquired the nickname "Rat" by chance: he had earned it.

Five years ago, when Scott was fourteen, he had entered a race by using an older friend's birth certificate. He was caught and disqualified, but not until several days after the race was over.

Another time he had used nitrous oxide in his gas, an offense in all racing classes and categories except Top Fuel and AA/Funny cars. He had told the officials he hadn't known it wasn't allowed. But every other drag racer had known it. Why hadn't he? There wasn't a soul in the racing crowd who didn't believe that Scott Taggart had lied through his teeth.

You would think that Dana, who had told all this to Ken one night about a year ago after he and

Scott had been biking together for a couple of hours, would have dropped Scott like a hot potato. But, no. They still chummed around, although not as much as they used to.

Anyway, Scott had been disqualified repeatedly in races all over the county. One time a member of the racing clan dubbed him with the nickname "Rat." And it had stuck ever since.

Ken heard a car drive up as he approached his pickup, but he didn't look around at it. He didn't want anyone to see the dismal expression on his face.

But a voice called out his name and he paused, feeling he had to look up now. He glanced at the car as it swept around in a quick turn and pulled up in the vacant space two cars away from his. It was a black, two-door Plymouth owned by no one else but the person he had just been thinking about, Scott "Rat" Taggart.

But it wasn't Scott's voice that had called to him. It was the voice of the girl sitting beside him — pretty, dark-haired Dottie Hill, Dusty's seventeen-year-old daughter.

"Oh, hi," he said, at the same time thinking, *What in heck is she doing with him?*

He let a frown linger on his face, remembering the two times he had taken her to the movies, and the few times he had danced with her at school functions. Then he turned away, opened the door of the pickup, put in the crutches, and got in.

He started the pickup and headed for home, embittered by the thought of Dusty's signing as a sponsor for Scott "Rat" Taggart. Well, he couldn't deny that Scott was a good driver. He had scored a lot of points in Pro Stock races — although he had never come in better than third runner-up — and had several trophies to show for it. Dusty, no greenhorn in the business, must have known a competitor when he saw one.

Ken wondered what to do to ease the pain of Dusty's turning him down and thought of going to a movie. But that was out. The theaters in Wade didn't open till one-thirty.

There was really only one place that would do — the Candlewyck Speedway — and he promptly headed for it. He got there in half an hour, parked next to the bleachers, and for the next hour and a half he watched the Plymouths, Omnis, Chevies, Mustangs, Camaros, Hornets, Fords, Buicks, Oldses, Pontiacs, and a bristling white Chrysler run passes on the quarter-mile strip.

"Snakeman" Wilkins was in a Plymouth, "Little Beaver" Applejack in a Mustang, "Battle-scar" Jones in a Ford, Jim "The Toad" in an Olds.

Their names were printed in glowing colors across the sides of their cars, which themselves were painted in sharp, contrasting colors. The first thing you noticed about these cars was their owners' pride in how they looked. And then, the way each car reflected the personality of its owner. Ken wondered if someday he'd be worthy enough to have earned a nickname and join that reputable clan. "Limp-along" Oberlin? "Wolfman" Oberlin? The possibilities were limitless.

Dana was in the backyard working on his motorcycle when Ken finally went home. He was bare to his waist and his hands were black from grease and oil.

"Nick give you the day off?" Ken found himself asking as he hobbled over to his brother.

Dana straightened and shoved his long hair away from his forehead with the clean part of his arm. "I'm taking it off, brother. Where you been?"

"At the track. But I went to see Dusty Hill first."

Dana eyed him expectantly. "What's the verdict?"

"He's already sponsoring a driver." Their eyes held. "Scott Taggart."

"Rat? Since when?"

Ken shrugged. "Since two days ago. Another thing: somebody broke into Dusty's place last night or early this morning and stole that three-fifty turbo engine he had sitting in his store."

"Oh, no." Dana shook his head sympathetically, then narrowed his eyes as he grasped the full impact of what Ken had said.

"Early this morning?"

"Yes, or last night."

"Hm," Dana muttered, shaking his head. Then he resumed work on his black and red Kawasaki, a KE125 model. The Takasago steel rims and Nitto tires were as clean and sparkling as if he had just bought them off the assembly line.

"See ya," Ken said, noticing that his brother seemed more interested in working on his bike than talking with him. Then a movement caught his eye toward the rear of their yard. He grinned amiably as he saw his father hoeing the garden. Dad was wearing that wide-brimmed, tattered straw hat that he had had for as long as Ken could remember.

The girls weren't around. They were probably in the house or playing with some of their neighborhood friends, Ken thought.

He hobbled to the garden to talk with his

44

father, and wasn't there more than ten minutes when he heard the Kawasaki start up. Surprised, he turned and saw Dana tearing away on it, dirt squirting up like sparks behind its rear wheel.

FIVE

FIVE MILES out of Wade, Dana turned off
the highway onto a road that was flanked on
one side by a cow pasture and on the other by tall,
gangling palms. He reduced the speed of his
motorcycle almost to idle so that the noise
wouldn't carry to the small ranch house nestled
about an eighth of a mile off the road among a
thick set of trees.

Some one hundred yards from the highway the
dirt road curved to the left, sweeping around a
tall, sprawling grapefruit tree.

Dana drove off the road to the left side of the
tree, shut off the engine, dismounted, and leaned
the motorcycle against the tree. Weeds were
chest-high around the tree and he doubted that
anyone who happened to drive by could see the
bike.

He ran across the road, hopped over a ditch, ducked through a wire fence, and headed toward a garage that was set away from the house.

He kept bent over, not wanting to risk having someone at the house see him. He knew of at least five shotguns kept inside that he had seen with his own eyes, with the shells for each of them easily available.

A green pickup and an old Dodge were parked in the driveway. Both had rust scales on the fenders, but the Dodge looked worse. Its front right fender was battered and the front door on the same side was caved in.

Dana reached a side window of the garage and peeked in. He had to wipe the dirt off the glass to see through it, but it didn't take long for him to spot the suspicious-looking tarpaulin-covered pile set on a couple of planks near the rear of the garage. He grabbed the wooden parts of the window and tried to force it open. It wouldn't budge.

He stood awhile, wondering what to do to get inside. He had to see what was underneath that tarpaulin.

Well, why not try the door? he thought. If he just kept down and out of sight, he should be able to make it.

He ducked low as he scurried to the front of

the garage, peeked around its corner, saw no one, and turned the knob of the door. For a scant second he was afraid it might be locked, although it never was, not whenever he'd been here.

He pushed the door and it slowly opened. He entered quickly and closed the door quietly behind him. Then he headed toward the rear of the building. The smell of grease and oil was thick in the air. The garage was like an automotive parts store, except that the parts were old and used and left haphazardly all over the place.

He reached the hidden bulge on the planks and felt tension begin to creep through his body as he grabbed an edge of the canvas and lifted it. His expectations were realized as he unveiled a brand-new engine. He read the HP on the head, 350, and then looked for the ID.

He found the place where it was supposed to be, but the numbers were gone. Filed off.

Dana pursed his lips. "Rat" really deserved his nickname, he thought. And my family calls *me* a black sheep! I'm a kitten compared to Scott "Rat" Taggart.

Last night he had stayed at the pool parlor shooting pool and guzzling beer with a couple of guys after work. Nick had wanted him to stay till midnight, at which hour he had promised to return from an appointment and take over till closing.

Instead, Nick didn't return till 2 A.M., which was okay with Dana. It was more money in his pocket and he had nothing else to do, anyway.

Then, while he was heading for home on his Kawasaki, breezing down Palmetto Avenue, he had seen a pickup pull up into a lane that led to the rear entrance to the stores of Wade Mall. It could've been brown, blue, or green — any of the dark colors — exactly which he couldn't swear for sure. He could hardly see the driver who, he remembered now as he thought back to that moment, had seemed to duck back against his seat. In the night shadows next to him sat a couple of passengers, both of whom had tried to keep out of his sight, too, now that he thought of it.

But the white sign on the door was plain: HILL's AUTO PARTS.

Dusty's working late, he had told himself. Or was it Rooster?

But that pickup looked different. Wasn't Dusty's white?

One other thing had caught his attention, but had not sufficiently registered at the time. The first three letters on the license plate: SRT.

There was only one person he knew whose

license plate started with those letters. Scott "Rat" Taggart. In spite of the connotation in the name "Rat," Scott was proud enough to use it in his initials.

But the letters had not meant anything to Dana at the time. Not until Ken had told him about the theft of the engine had the pictures of a puzzle begun to fall into place. Seconds later, while Ken was out there in the garden shooting the breeze with his father, Dana had gone to the telephone and called up Dusty to check out the color of his pickup. It was white, Dusty had told him. And when Dusty had wanted to know who was calling, Dana had simply said, "A friend."

As for the "Hill's Auto Parts" sign, it didn't take a genius to paint one and tape it to the side of a pickup.

He pulled the tarpaulin back over the engine and headed out of the garage, careful to crack the door open and peek out before he made his departure.

The coast was clear. He hurried around to the side of the garage and then back through the brush to his motorcycle, feeling good that his hunch was right. He had never considered Scott a real friend, anyway — he had never felt he could trust the guy. This dirty business of Scott's stealing an engine from Dusty Hill at about the same time that Dusty had agreed to sponsor him in races was proof that he was exactly what his nickname said: a rat.

Dana finally reached the spot at the side of the ditch that was directly across from the tree against which he had propped his motorcycle. Glancing again toward the house to make sure no one was watching him, he sprinted across the road.

Just as he got to the tree, a figure rose out of the tall weeds. Dana froze as he found himself staring at the cold, deadly end of a double-barreled shotgun.

"Hold it right there, young fella," said the scrawny, thin-faced man pointing the gun at him. "I can shoot you, you know, for trespassing on my property!"

Dana peered into the narrowed, beady eyes over which lay a thatch of tousled, wheat-colored hair. "You'd better think twice about that, Mr. Taggart," he warned. "I'm a friend of Scott's, and you'd have a hard time telling the cops whatever it is you've got in mind."

"I saw you sneak up to my garage," Scott's father snarled. "What were you looking for?"

"You know darn well what I was looking for," Dana snapped.

The old man eyed him warily. "How'd you find out about it?"

"What's the difference? The fact is I know about the engine," Dana said. "Stealing an engine isn't going to look a bit good for your sons, is it?"

"Don't talk to me like you're an angel, young fella," Mr. Taggart snorted. "Your reputation ain't one to brag about."

"But I have never stolen, Mr. Taggart," said Dana. "I'm no angel, but I'm no thief, either. That's a department where your boys got one over on me." He grinned wryly as he watched the old man's eyes glitter with anger.

"Scott figured on using that engine in a car he was going to race for Mr. Hill," Mr. Taggart explained. "Then, if he started winning, he was going to tell Mr. Hill the truth."

"I guess I look like a dumbbell to you, don't I, Mr. Taggart?" said Dana patiently. "Know what? I think you'd better tell your boys to return that engine to Dusty Hill; otherwise they might be finding themselves in jail. Tell them to have it back within the next two hours, Mr. Taggart."

The gun wavered as the old man looked at him, frowning, as if wondering what to say to the ultimatum.

Dana took a step forward, then another and another until he was near the motorcycle. From the corner of his eye he could see the barrel of the gun follow his movements, but he had a strong hunch that Mr. Taggart wouldn't pull the trigger. A stolen engine wasn't worth the price of murder, Dana told himself, and he hoped old man Taggart had sense enough to realize that.

While part of him was gripped with fear, and another part of him told him there was nothing to worry about, he grabbed the handlebars of the Kawasaki and pushed it gently through the brush onto the road. Gingerly, he turned the machine to face the highway beyond, then got on it, kicked the starter, and rode away. Breathlessly he waited for that one-in-a-million chance that Mr. Taggart, in a moment of sudden desperation, would pull the trigger. But the shot wasn't fired.

Dana reached the highway, then drove into town to the Wade Mall.

He found Dusty Hill waiting on a pair of customers, and hung around patiently until they were taken care of and had left.

Dusty wrote something on the front left side of the cash register, then put down the pencil and looked at Dana. "Hi, Dana. What can I do for you?"

"A lot, Dusty," Dana said, and he went on to

tell Dusty what Ken had told him about the theft of the 350-HP turbo engine and that he knew, and could prove, who had stolen it.

Dusty eyed him suspiciously. "Were you the one who called me up and asked about the color of my pickup?"

Dana nodded.

"Okay, who?" Dusty wanted to know. "And how do you know?"

"I'll tell you," Dana said, "if you promise to sponsor Ken in his races."

Dusty's eyebrows arched. "Now, wait a minute," he said. "In the first place I can't see how a sixteen-year-old kid with a cast on one leg can be such a hot driver on a drag strip."

"That cast is on his left leg and it isn't hindering him one bit," Dana told him. "Neither is his age. He's been driving in our backyard since he was fourteen years old. And, since his sixteenth birthday, he's been driving that little red car almost every day to gain all the experience he could. He's already driven it in autocrosses. I'd put him up against older drivers any day of the week, Dusty. I know my brother. He can drive."

Dusty smiled slowly. "Well, you should know, shouldn't you?"

Yes, I should; and I do, Dana thought. Even

though, at first, he had wished Uncle Louis had bequeathed the car to him.

The seconds dragged as he waited for Dusty to give him a definite answer. Finally Dusty broke the silence. "I'm surprised Ken didn't tell you. I'm already sponsoring a driver. Scott Taggart."

"He did tell me. But, if you promise you'll sponsor Ken, I promise you won't ever bother with Scott Taggart again. Not ever."

Their eyes met.

Dusty looked at his fingernails, picked at one, then looked up at Dana. "Okay, Dana. I promise. Who's got the engine?"

Relief swept over Dana. "There's one more thing, Dusty, before I tell you," he said.

"What's that?"

"I don't want Ken to know that I've told you this."

"Why not?"

Dana shrugged. "He's proud, that's why. If he found that I'd gone out of my way to trace who stole that engine and asked you to sponsor him in races, he'd feel as if he had to be indebted to me for the rest of his life. I don't want that."

Dusty nodded. "Okay. It'll be just between you and me."

"Thanks. That engine of yours is sitting in

Scott Taggart's father's garage," Dana said evenly. "And the guy who stole it out of your shop here is Scott Taggart himself. With the help of his two brothers, of course."

Dusty's eyes widened, and he seemed to stiffen for a moment as if Dana's words had hit him like buckshot.

"Can you prove it?" he said.

"I promised his father," Dana explained, "that if they brought that engine back within the next two hours they wouldn't have to worry about going to jail."

Suddenly sparks of anger danced in Dusty's eyes. "You double-crossed me, Dana. You tricked me into making that promise when I would have found out anyway."

Dana's mouth parted in a slow grin. "You won't be sorry, Dusty, I promise. Ken's going to turn out to be one of the best drivers in the state. He's determined."

Dusty's mouth tightened. "You expect me to let Taggart get away with it?"

"You've got to this time, Dusty. I'm probably darned lucky I'm alive and standing here talking to you. Old man Taggart had a gun pointed at my chest all the time I was talking with him."

Dusty studied Dana's face for a few moments

as if to see whether there might be a trace of a lie in what he had said. Then, apparently satisfied, he agreed not to tell the cops.

"But," he added, "if Scott doesn't have the engine back in two hours I will call them. If he was so darned white-livered that he'd steal an engine two days after I agreed to sponsor him in his races, he'd be white-livered enough to try to hide it somewhere else, or dump it into a river."

"When are you going to call up Ken and tell him he's got the job?" Dana asked him.

"As soon as I see that engine with my own eyes," Dusty promised stiffly.

SIX

KEN WAS POLISHING Li'l Red late the following afternoon when he got a call from Dusty Hill. Dusty said he'd like Ken to come to the store just as soon as he was free.

"In about half an hour, all right, Mr. Hill?" Ken suggested. "I'm putting a polish on my car right now."

"Half an hour's fine," Dusty said.

Ken's hand shook with excitement as he hung up the receiver. What does Dusty want to see me about? he wondered. It had to do with drag racing, he was sure. But what about it? Dusty had already arranged to sponsor Scott Taggart. And, although Ken hated to admit it, Scott was a better driver than he. He had been running that 1320-foot strip so often he probably knew every little scar on it.

Ken finished polishing Li'l Red, then washed his hands, put on clean clothes, and drove to Dusty Hill's parts store in his pickup.

Dusty was alone, having a cup of coffee and a doughnut at his desk behind the cash register.

"Like some coffee?" Dusty offered. "Got a potful."

"I'm not a coffee man," Ken said.

"Then how about a doughnut?"

"Okay."

Dusty lifted a waxed-paper sack up to the glass display counter behind which Ken stood, and Ken took one out. He bit into it, his teeth sinking into the soft, tasty morsel, and wondered how long he'd have to wait before Dusty told him why he wanted to see him.

Suddenly his eyes caught sight of a new engine at the rear of the store.

"See you've got another engine, Mr. Hill," he said.

Dusty shook his head. "No. It's the same one I had before."

Ken stopped chewing the doughnut for a minute. "The cops find it?"

"No. The thieves brought it back themselves. Or, I should say, the thief, with his brothers' help.

Someone — well, someone caught them stealing it and told them they'd better return it or else."

Ken frowned, his mind spinning in higher gear. "Has that engine got anything to do with your wanting to see me?"

Dusty smiled. "I think you've got it."

"Scott Taggart steal the engine?"

"You've got it again. It was Taggart — and his brothers. I guess his nickname, 'Rat,' suits him to a T."

Ken found it difficult to swallow the piece of doughnut he had in his mouth. What gall Taggart must have, he thought, to steal an engine from the guy who was going to sponsor him.

Dusty wiped his mouth with a paper napkin. "Anyway, now that he's out of the picture, I'd like to sponsor you in at least two or three races. See how you run."

Ken was instantly bubbling with excitement. "It would be a pleasure, Mr. Hill."

He extended his hand, and Dusty got off his chair and shook it. Ken had a hard time restraining himself. This was what he needed, a sponsor like Dusty Hill to back him up with tires and parts for his machine whenever he needed them, and money for the entry fees. Racing was a joy, but it was no picnic without backing and the green stuff.

They discussed and agreed on an arrangement, Dusty to receive forty percent of the winnings in exchange for taking care of the car's repairs and Ken's entry fees in the races. Dusty put it all down on paper, then both signed it. Dusty handed a copy of it to Ken and kept the original.

Ken happily folded his copy and was ready to put it into his pocket when the door clanged open. He glanced toward it, and his heart gave a slight leap as he saw Dottie.

She paused in front of the door as their eyes met. She seemed surprised to see him, and it was a few seconds before she spoke. "Hi, Ken. How are you?"

"Hi, Dottie. I'm fine, now."

She closed the door gently behind her, then started forward, her blue eyes flicking perplexedly from him to her father and back to him. "Now? What does that mean?"

"I'm going to sponsor him in two or three races," her father explained. "I've fired Scott Taggart."

She froze. "Fired him? Why?"

Her father turned and pointed at the engine sitting on a mount near the back of the store. "He was the one who stole that engine. If someone hadn't seen him and made him bring it back, I would never have known that I was sponsoring a crook's racing car."

Dottie's face turned beet red. Then she spun around and flounced out of the store, her heels clicking on the hard wood floor. For a moment Ken thought that Dusty might try to call her back, but he didn't.

The door slammed shut behind her, and they watched her as she walked past the wide display window, her strides long and deliberate. A little while later they heard a car start up, its motor racing madly for a second or two. Then they heard it drive off, its exhaust roaring.

"Don't mind her," Dusty said easily. "She's hurt and confused. I guess she had taken a liking to Taggart."

Ken didn't answer. What she had seen in the guy must be something only she could explain.

He shook hands again with Dusty, promising he'd try never to let him down, then left.

He arrived home and found Dana outside of the garage, talking with two guys straddling their motorcycles. One was a stranger to him. The other, the one with the heavy eyebrows and a mustache, was Nick Evans.

His jaw tightened at the sight of Nick. He

didn't trust the guy as far as he could throw a bull. He wished Dana would quit working for him.

They spoke briefly, and Nick asked him how his foot was. He said it was okay and walked toward the house, conscious of their eyes watching him. Sensing their eyes on him made him nervous, and just before he reached the step leading up to the porch, the rubber foot of his right-hand crutch landed on a pebble and slipped off, causing him to lose his balance.

He caught himself in time and headed up the porch, blushing at the near mishap. Darn the crutches, he thought. The sooner he got rid of them the better.

He was anxious to tell Dana that Dusty Hill had changed his mind and was going to sponsor him, but he felt he had to wait till Dana was alone.

His mother was fixing supper and the girls were helping her. He sat down, leaning the crutches against the wall behind him, before he broke the good news to them.

"Hey," his mother said, her eyes brightening. "I guess he knows a good driver when he sees one, doesn't he?"

Ken grinned. Was she having a change of heart about his racing ambitions?

He didn't say anything about Scott Taggart. Not even about the engine Scott had stolen and returned. But he still wondered who had seen him taking it.

"You see those guys out there with your brother?" his mother said. "The one with the mustache is Nick Evans. Frankly, I don't trust him, and I wish that Dana wouldn't work for him in his pool parlor, or chum around with him. I've told Dana, but I might as well talk to that wall."

Ken picked up a crutch and limped over to the refrigerator. "Don't worry about him, Mom. Dana's old enough to take care of himself."

"Age doesn't make any difference when you run around with the wrong kind of people," she replied. She turned to look at him where she was standing by the electric range, stirring macaroni in a large aluminum kettle. "Can't you wait another few minutes? Dinner will be on the table soon."

"Just want a drink of iced tea, Mom," he told her.

SEVEN

TIME TO EAT, Dana!" Janet called to him from the porch. "It's already on the table!"

"Be right there!" he answered her. He turned to Nick and Phil Bettix, a guy he had just met. "See you at the hall. Okay?"

They nodded, then started up their motorcycles and took off. Dana watched Nick's twin-carbed 250cc Kawasaki sprint away down the driveway and then down the street like a young colt full of spit and vinegar. Bettix's black and white Honda had a slow start, but the minute he had it on the street he goosed its engine and started to close the gap quickly between himself and Nick.

Dana smiled at their game, then turned and headed toward the house.

65

Anxious to know how Ken's meeting with Dusty came out, he was barely able to restrain himself from asking Ken about it. He didn't want Ken to have the slightest notion that it was he who was responsible for the meeting.

His concern and anxiety didn't last. Ken told him the news almost before Dana had closed the door behind him.

"Congratulations, brother!" Dana said, and shook Ken's hand. "What made him change his mind?"

"Someone had seen Scott Taggart and his brothers steal the engine," Ken explained, "and made Scott promise to take it back or expect to be arrested. Dusty didn't say, but probably Scott paid the guy not to squeal to the cops."

"It's possible," Dana said steadily. "Anyway, I'm glad you got Dusty to sponsor you. He's a good man to have backing you up."

After dinner he excused himself and took off on his Kawasaki for Nick's pool parlor. His mother's pale blue eyes hovered in his mind as he barreled the motorcycle down the street, the warm wind whistling past the plastic shield of his helmet. He knew she wasn't crazy about his spending so much time at the parlor and in Nick Evans's company, but the job was his bread and butter. And he liked the crowd that came to play pool. They *weren't* all roughnecks and trouble-makers as she had said they were. Once in a while one or two guys with a little too much to drink might start a quarrel, but, in general, most of the patrons were nice, law-abiding guys and girls.

"For crying out loud, Ma," he had said to her, "you seem to think that only bad kids hang around pool halls. There are a lot of good kids that hang around them, too."

He didn't think he had convinced her.

He reached Nick's place, parked his motor-cycle, locked it, and strode into the building with the helmet under his arm.

He had a beer, then he found Nick and Bettix at one of the tables and joined them.

They were in the middle of a game when Nick asked him, "Well, is Dusty going to sponsor Ken?"

Dana watched Phil Bettix lean his tall, thin frame over his cue stick and size up his next shot. "He is," he said.

"Good. Maybe he'd be interested in a proposi-tion I've got to offer him."

Dana looked at him. "What do you mean?"

"I mean that racing can pay off for him in more ways than one."

Dana's eyes studied him a few moments while butterflies started to flutter in his stomach.

"Maybe you should have told him that you would sponsor him," he said.

"I'm not about to sponsor anybody," Nick answered tersely. "Not just yet, anyway."

Phil shot and drove the number-two ball into a corner pocket.

"He won't throw a race, Nick," Dana said, getting to the point. "My kid brother is too darn honest to pull a thing like that."

Nick chuckled. "I've met a lot of honest kids in my day, Dana. Most of them have a little bit of larceny in that honest-to-goodness heart of theirs. He's your blood brother. You can't make me believe that a little bit of you isn't in him. And that powerful green stuff, money, will bring it out of him."

Dana watched Phil miss a side-pocket shot by half an inch. But his ears were tuned in to what Nick Evans was saying, and he could hardly believe what he heard.

Time passed as if in slow motion. He watched Nick walk around the table to get in position for a shot on the eleven ball. Nick didn't play often; only when there were about two or three people in the room. Most of the time he lingered near the cash register, watching the players or reading a magazine.

Nick made the shot, but the cream-colored ball ricocheted against the cushion, then rolled back across the table into a side pocket.

Bettix picked the eleven ball out of the pocket, spotted it on the white dot, then got the cue ball and set it in position.

"Tell Ken to give me a call," Nick said. "No rush. It can be at his convenience." He glanced toward the doorway where four customers were just entering. "Here. Finish the game." He handed the cue stick to Dana and walked toward the front of the room to take care of them.

Bettix, still leaning over the table with the small end of the cue stick poked through his looped forefinger, said softly, "Don't underestimate Nick, my friend. I've known him a long time. He gambles, and seldom loses. Even when it comes to predicting people."

He shot. The cue ball struck the three ball on the side, angling it straight toward the corner pocket. The ball dropped in.

But the cue ball hadn't finished its job. It hit the far side of the table, then ricocheted sharply to the left and kissed the five ball that stood near the corner pocket.

Bettix went on to clean the table.

Dana stared at him, incredulous. "Hey, who are you, anyway?" he asked.

Bettix smiled. "Head mechanic at Troy's Garage, and one heck of a lucky pool player. Come on. I'll buy you a beer."

EIGHT

THE PHONE woke Ken. It rang and rang, and he began to wonder if there was anyone else in the house.

Presently he heard footsteps hurrying across the floor, then the ringing stopped. Seconds later there was a tap on his door.

"Ken, are you awake?" It was his mother's voice. She sounded worried.

He flipped back the covers. "Yeah," he said.

"Dana's on the phone. He wants to talk to you."

Dana? What does he want? "Be right there," he said.

He turned on the lamp that stood on the night-stand next to his bed and glanced at the small, radium-dialed clock sitting next to it. Quarter of

71

three. Oh, man, he thought. Now what was Dana up to?

He reached for his crutches and hobbled out of the room.

The light in the hall was lit. It created a soft glow around his mother's head as she stood there in front of it, her face slightly in shadow.

"He says he's all right, but what's he doing out this late at night?" she said worriedly. "And why should he be asking for you?"

Ken hobbled past her. "Go back to bed, Mom," he said. "I'm sure he's all right. If he wasn't, it would've been someone else calling."

It was a lame statement, he knew, and he didn't think he was fooling her one bit. But he had to say something and that was the best thing he could think of right now.

He got to the phone and picked it up. "This is Ken," he said.

"Ken, I'm in the brig," Dana said. "I had an accident with my bike and they got me on a DUI."

"Great; driving under the influence, really smart," said Ken, feeling a stab of disgust. "What do you want me to do?"

"Bail me out, what else? It's only two hundred

dollars. But I don't want anybody else in the family to know about this."

Ken glanced back over his shoulder and saw his mother staring at him from the next room.

"Dana, I haven't got two hundred dollars," he said, lowering his voice. "I've put all I had in that car. You know that."

"I know, I know," said Dana. He didn't sound drunk to Ken. "Ask Dusty Hill for it. I'm sure he'll give it to you."

"I can't ask him. I haven't even raced for him yet. What about Nick Evans?"

"No, not Nick," countered Dana. "Look, see Dusty..."

"Why not Nick?" Ken interrupted. "You work for him. Why wouldn't he put up bail for you?"

He heard Dana take a deep breath and let it out. "I don't want Nick involved in this, Ken," he said irritably. "That's final. Keep his name out of this. See Dusty. He'll give it to you. Tell him I'll pay him back in a month or so. But, for crying out loud, do it as soon as you can this morning. I don't want to stay in this hoosegow all day."

Ken sighed. "Okay, Dana. I'll see what I can do."

He hung up.

He turned slowly, hoping his mother wasn't still back there waiting for him. But she was. Her eyes were wide with anxiety, her face like dough in the weak light.

"He's in trouble, isn't he?" she murmured.

He hobbled toward her, then started to go past her. "He was in a small accident," he said uneasily. "He isn't hurt, though, so don't worry."

She laid a hand on his arm. "Where is he?"

He hesitated. "Mom, he's all right. Don't worry about him."

He walked past her, feeling her eyes piercing his back.

"Ken," she said.

He paused and turned around. "He's in jail, Mom, under two-hundred-dollar bail," he explained. "I'm going to ask Dusty Hill for the money this morning to bail him out."

He felt he had to tell her. He couldn't let her go to bed worrying the worst about Dana.

"If I had it — " she started to say.

"But you don't," Ken cut in, "so forget it. Go to bed. It'll work out."

He went back to bed himself, staring up at the darkened ceiling. That brother of mine, he

74

thought. What is it going to be the next time? A real smashup in which he'd barely survive? Or didn't survive?

It was ten of eight, and his father was already sitting down at breakfast when Ken entered the kitchen. Ken could tell immediately from the expression on his father's face that he had learned about Dana.

He sat down and had a glass of orange juice while his mother started to cook some hot cereal for him.

"So your brother finally got jailed on a DUI charge," his father broke the awkward silence. "I'd let him sit there for a couple of days. Let him get some sense into that crazy head of his."

Ken stared at him.

"Frank!" Mrs. Oberlin exclaimed. "He's your son! How can you say a thing like that? Why, he'd be more hurt than ever — "

"Hurt?" her husband cut in, looking up at her. "How about me? And you? Aren't you hurt about what happened to him, and what he keeps doing to mess up his life? Maybe a couple of days in jail will be just the thing to teach him a lesson or two."

"Don't say that, Dad," Ken said. "He already

thinks you don't care what happens to him. And that you don't love him. If he could hear what you're saying now — " He paused. "Well, I don't know what he'd do."

"If I didn't love him I wouldn't care what happened to him," his father grunted. "And the same goes for you."

For a moment their eyes met, and Ken felt a desperate urge to reach over and touch his father's hand. But just then his mother came over with the cereal and poured it into the bowl in front of him.

After his mother had left for work, Ken left to run his errand, knowing that Dana must be sitting on pins and needles in that jail cell waiting for him to arrive with the bail money.

He drove the pickup to the Wade Mall and found Dusty having coffee and doughnuts with Rooster. They both looked at him as he stepped into the store, and for a minute he wondered if he should mention his mission to Dusty in front of Rooster.

Anyway, Dusty didn't ask what brought him here so early. Instead, he offered Ken a doughnut which Ken accepted.

They talked briefly about his leg. "You're walking with those crutches as if you've always had 'em," Rooster said. They talked about his little red racing car. "Race coming up this Saturday. You going to enter it?" the mechanic wanted to know.

Ken said no, he wasn't. He wanted to run more passes with the car.

Would he be ready to race next weekend? He wasn't sure, he said.

Rooster finally finished his second doughnut and his coffee, ran a hand across his mouth to wipe off the rim of powdered sugar, and left. The minute the door clanged shut behind him, Ken began to steel himself against the embarrassment of asking Dusty for the money to bail Dana out of jail. They had signed an agreement that Dusty would back him up in three successive races, with the option for more races should they find that their partnership was mutually satisfactory. But Ken still didn't feel close enough to Dusty to ask him for two hundred dollars to bail out Dana without alligators prowling around in his stomach.

"Something on your mind, Ken?" Dusty asked, wiping the cup out with a napkin and then setting it on a shelf next to the coffee maker.

"Yeah."

Thoughts jumbled in his mind for a few seconds before he finally got them together. "I need two hundred dollars to bail my brother out of jail."

Dusty's eyes widened with surprise. "What did he do?"

"He got into an accident with his motorcycle and was arrested for drunken driving."

"Did he get hurt?"

"No."

Dusty sucked in a deep breath, pursed his lips, and shook his head. Ken interpreted it to mean that Dusty was refusing him. But then Dusty leaned over to one side, took out his wallet, and picked out two fifty-dollar bills. He got two more fifties out of the cash register and handed them all over to Ken.

Ken felt his hand tremble as he took them. "Thanks, Mr. Hill. I hadn't wanted to ask you, but — "

"Forget it. Always willing to help a friend."

"Thanks again. Dana promised he'd pay you back within a month. If he doesn't, well . . . I'll try to myself. I'll sign an IOU if you want me to."

Dusty raised his hand. "Hey. Forget it. I'll take your brother's word that he'll pay me back. He's not all that bad." The last sentence came out almost as an afterthought.

Ken stuck the two hundred dollars into his wallet, said good-bye to Dusty, and walked out of the store.

Within twenty minutes Dana was out of jail.

In the pickup Dana said, "Dusty gave you the money, didn't he?"

"Yeah."

Dana reached over and squeezed Ken's knee. "I appreciate this, brother."

"Well, you owe him two hundred. I told him you had promised to pay him back in a month."

"Don't worry," Dana said easily. "I will."

On the following Monday Ken hauled Li'l Red to the Candlewyck Speedway in hopes of running a dozen or so passes with her. This time both Janet and Lori rode with him. Lori hadn't seen him drive the little red Chevy down any speedway track yet and had begged to go along.

He got the surprise of his life when he got out of the pickup and started to pull down the ramp on the trailer. He had heard a voice over the public address system and looked up to see someone waving to him from a window of the timing tower.

"Oberlin, I'm sorry, but you can't run your car on the track," came Buck Morrison's ringing voice.

Ken stiffened. "Why not?" he shouted.

There was a pause. Then the face disappeared from the window.

His sisters stared at him. Janet looked shocked and surprised, and Lori sadly disappointed.

"Get into the truck," Ken said, his jaw set.

They piled in. He got behind the wheel and drove up to the timing tower. His heart was pumping hard as he grabbed his crutches and stepped out of the truck.

"I'll be right back," he said.

He entered the building at the rear of which another door led to the lanes. Inside were wind- and rain-battered signs regarding racing dates, coils of cords and electric bulbs hung haphazardly up on the walls, and the electronic starting device — the Christmas tree — standing on a tripod near the center of the wood floor.

Ken started up the steps that ran along the wall. A shadow moved across the wall and he glanced up to see Buck Morrison looking down at him over the upstairs railing. Then the shadow vanished as Buck moved away.

When Ken finally reached the second floor he saw Buck sitting at his desk, reading one of the letters piled on it. Jay Wells was on a phone at

another desk and a girl was banging on a typewriter at a third desk.

Between Buck's and Jay's desks were the public
address system units and the console from which
the Christmas tree was operated.

For almost a minute Ken stood there and no one
seemed to notice him, even though Buck had seen
him ascending the stairs only moments before.
The only sounds in the room were the staccato
tap-tap-tap of the typewriter and the soft country
music emanating from a portable radio.

"Excuse me," Ken said.

Buck and Jay turned and looked at him. The
girl kept pounding on the typewriter.

"Good morning, Mr. Oberlin," Buck Morrison said.

"Morning." Ken felt a tightening in his stomach. "Why can't I use the track?"

Ken saw Buck flash a glance at his partner.
Then he looked back at Ken. "For starters, we
figured that it was best you didn't until you got
that cast off your leg."

"I've driven that car with the cast on, Mr. Morrison," Ken said firmly. "You know I have. And
the cast is on my left leg. It doesn't hinder me one
bit."

Buck shrugged. "We see it differently, Mr. Oberlin."

He turned and picked up another letter from the pile in front of him.

"I don't think you're doing this because of the cast," Ken said, trying to control his anger. "I think there's some other reason. What do you mean, 'for starters'?"

The two partners looked at each other again, and Ken felt a message being exchanged between them. Then Buck turned back to him and said, "We received a phone call that at least two guys won't race if you're going to race, too."

Ken frowned. "Why not? What did I do?"

Buck cleared his throat, "This person swore that you'd been drinking before you got in the accident that resulted in your breaking that leg," he said tersely. "We just can't take a chance that it'll happen again, Mr. Oberlin."

Ken stared at him. "Drinking? That's a darn lie! My brakes blew! Who told you I was drinking?"

"I'm sorry, Mr. Oberlin," Buck said, and turned back to his work.

Ken grabbed his shoulder. Buck whirled, his eyes furious. "You heard me! I'm *sorry!* Now, will you excuse me? We're all very busy."

"Yeah," Ken said, glancing at Jay Wells and the girl again. "I can see that very well."

He bit down hard on his lower lip to keep his emotions under control, then walked back downstairs and got into the pickup.

The girls wanted to know why he couldn't use the track and he told them only a part of what Morrison had told him; he said it was because of the cast on his leg.

He didn't want them to worry unduly over him.

NINE

KEN WRACKED HIS BRAIN trying to think of a place to practice driving his car. They were on the highway heading back toward Wade, but he didn't feel like returning home just yet.

Only the buzzing drone of the Ford's engine and the hum of the tires on the road cut into the otherwise silent cab of the pickup. They passed by fields of short-cropped grass, feathery-foliaged jacaranda trees, and tall, single-trunked palms. It was while passing a field in which cattle grazed, placidly ignoring the white egrets that stood on their backs feasting on bugs, that Ken thought of a place. The field just north of here, off Lychee Road. An old abandoned airport.

A smile creased his face as he stepped on the gas

and sped to the junction where Lychee Road turned off the highway. Four miles farther on they were there.

He stopped the truck in front of the gate leading onto the field, gazed at the weather-beaten hangar and the black-topped runway, which had begun to sprout stubbles of grass, and smiled again. "Perfect!" he exclaimed. "Now if we can get permission to use it."

He turned the truck around and drove to a small ranch house about a mile back. The man who answered his knock was the abandoned airport's owner. Ken kept his mental fingers crossed as he asked for permission to drive his car on the runway. He wouldn't be there more than half an hour, he promised.

The man — a tall, rotund figure in overalls — glanced past Ken's shoulder at the little red car sitting on the trailer and, without blinking an eye, said, "Sure, you can. It'll be the first time anything's been on that runway in five years."

Ken was instantly alight with excitement. "Thank you. Is the gate locked?"

"Just lift up the chain," the man told him.

Ken thanked him again, then returned to the truck and drove back down the road to the gate.

He got out, lifted the chain from the fence post, swung the gate open on groaning, rusty hinges, and drove in.

He parked beside the old building, which he could see now had part of a damaged airplane's fuselage inside of it. Then he unloaded the racer, put on his firesuit, helmet, and gloves, and drove the car onto the airstrip.

Sitting behind the wheel again filled him with excitement. The sound of the motor was like an eight-piece orchestra joined in perfect harmony, and he was the man with the baton.

He nodded to his sisters, who were standing by the pickup, watching him with eager faces.

Then he pulled back the gear lever and stepped on the gas. He pushed the pedal down only about two-thirds of the way. He didn't want to start off with full power just yet. Treat it kindly the first two or three times, he figured, then put the pressure on it.

The Chevy leaped forward without a hint of hesitation, each piston responding like a musician the instant the baton signaled the command.

Ken then pressed the accelerator to the floor and felt the car take off under him. Cracks in the runway made the ride slightly rough.

He let up on the gas pedal and decided to pay

more attention to the surface of the road than to his driving. Hitting one bad pothole could blow a tire, buckle a suspension rod, or damage a frame; so he wanted to take a good look at the runway before committing Li'l Red to it.

He drove the full length of the airstrip, figuring it was about three thousand feet long, and felt satisfied that it was safe to race the Chevy on it without fear of trouble.

He slowed down, made a U-turn at the end of the runway, then raced it back.

When he started off again he pretended that the Christmas tree was there in front of him, just slightly off to the right. He waited, mentally watching the lights flash on. Then — the green. And he stomped on the gas.

The Chevy shot forward like a sprinting colt. Its front end rose as if it were going to take off like an airplane. Then it settled down, and the speedometer climbed . . . 80 miles per hour . . . 85 . . . 90 . . . 95 . . .

The car went over the 100-mile-per-hour mark and Ken's face glowed with pride as he felt two tons of power answering to his command.

One hundred . . . 105 . . . 110. . . . The needle jumped forward as if it had gone crazy.

Then he slowed down, turned around, and

raced back, pleased with the Chevy's performance.

It wasn't till he reached the other end again, and
slowed down where his sisters and the pickup
were, that he realized that they had visitors. Two
men were standing on the other side of the fence
in front of a battered old car. They looked to be
in their sixties, wore nondescript pants and shirts,
and were bearded.

One of them began waving at him. Ken smiled
and waved back, although he wasn't sure it was
that kind of a wave.

He was right. The man began making other
gestures, and shaking his head vigorously.

"They don't want you to run your car here,
Ken," Janet said to him.

"What? Why not? It's not their property.
What are they beefing about?"

Ignoring them, he got back into position for another run. He stepped on the gas and again sped
down the runway.

This time he saw the speedometer needle move
up to the 115-mile-per-hour mark, and he was
pleased. But he could only guess at the time that
it had taken to reach that speed. It could've been
ten, eleven, or twelve seconds.

He made the U-turn, but this time drove back

slowly to the starting point. It seemed more natural now, even after only a couple of passes, to think of that end of the runway as the place from which to start.

He got into position again and paused to catch his breath. Then he heard a cry and glanced toward the girls. Both looked panic-stricken as they pointed behind them.

Ken looked toward the two men and stared in disbelief as he saw one of them pointing a shotgun at him. The other was pointing a finger at him and shouting, "Get that doggone car off'n the track or we'll puncture it with holes!"

Ken's jaw slackened. He wanted to pinch himself to see if he was dreaming. It was like a scene out of an old silent movie. One of those black-and-white Charlie Chaplin comedies he had seen on television that made him laugh so much.

But this was no laughing matter, he told himself. These characters were real. That gun was real.

"I got permission from the owner!" he shouted at them. "I'm not doing this illegally!"

"That ain't the point!" the skinny one on the left shouted back. "We're not going to stand for any more noise! That Francione guy knows that and should've told you! If you start using that field to drive your crazy, noisy car on it, the next thing we know the whole county will be using it! Why do you think we made them other people close up their airport for?"

Ken listened as if the words, too, were coming out of a TV set. He sat and stared at the man who had done the talking, then at the other, who had the gun trained on the car.

"Come on! Get that car out of here! We mean business, young fella, and if you don't believe it, just make another dash down that runway!"

Ken looked at them grimly. "I'll get the sheriff!" he yelled. "Then we'll see if I can use this runway or not!"

The men's raw-boned faces creased into smiles. "Go ahead," said the skinny one. "He'll tell you what he told the others. We got our rights. We're against noise pollution and we're the only ones who live close to this here field. So our word goes, young fella. If you don't believe it, go ahead. See the sheriff. But you'll only be wasting more gas. And with the price of it —"

Ken refused to hear any more, or become further involved with them. Their reasoning seemed crazy, but out here in the country, who knew what rules applied?

He drove the car back on the trailer, got out,

took off his gear, and told the girls to get into the truck. Then he got in himself and drove off the field.

He gave the men a final cold glance as he got out to put the chain over the fence. They were still standing there, as if to make sure he was really going to leave.

TEN

THIS TIME Ken headed for home. Offhand
he didn't know of another field he could run
passes on, anyway.

His whole body felt as if it had been inside a
sweatbox, and just removing the firesuit, gloves,
and helmet didn't make him feel much cooler.
The sun was still breathing hot air down on the
land and there wasn't enough breeze to stir a
feather. What he wanted more than anything
right now was a long, cool shower.

Most of the conversation on the way home was
between the girls, and all of it was about "those
two old dumb guys" with the gun. Lori said she
would've called the sheriff, no matter what they
had said.

"Isn't it a crime to threaten someone with a
gun?" she asked.

"I guess it is," Ken agreed. "But what if they had used it? The sheriff would surely be on their necks if that guy *had* shot and filled Li'l Red with holes, but they might have shot me, too, and I wasn't about to test their patience. I'd just as soon stay clear of people like them. I'll have to find another place to run Li'l Red, that's all."

They entered the city limits of Wade and were passing by Wade Mall when Ken recognized a familiar car coming toward him. It was a blue Toyota with white trim.

A second or two later it swung toward the curb and the driver began waving furiously at him. It was Dottie Hill.

He glanced quickly at his sideview mirror, then at the rearview mirror, and saw no car within fifty yards of him; so he drove to the curb on his side and stepped on the brake pedal. Rolling down his window, he called back to her, "Hi!"

"Hi!" she answered. "I'd like to see you! Can you stop at the coffee shop?"

"Sure!"

She smiled, ducked her head back into the car, and drove off. There was a driveway into the mall's parking lot a few yards farther down the street that she could turn into.

He checked the traffic again, found it clear, and

drove ahead till he reached the next area, where he made a left turn into the mall's parking lot.

What does she want? he wondered. The last time he remembered seeing her was at her father's auto parts store, when she had walked out in a huff after learning that her father had changed his mind about sponsoring Scott Taggart.

He parked the pickup in a vacant spot large enough to accommodate it and the trailer, then got out, lifted out his crutches, and headed toward the coffee shop. His mind was so preoccupied with Dottie Hill that he'd gone twenty feet before he remembered his sisters.

He turned, his face brick red, and motioned for them to come with him.

"You sure you want us to?" Janet called back to him, giving him a grin that embarrassed him even more.

"Sure, I'm sure," he said, smiling. "Come on."

Dottie was already in the coffee shop, sitting at a booth near the door. Her eyes sparkled at the sight of him and she moved farther in to make room for one of the girls.

Greetings were exchanged as Janet slid into the seat beside her. Lori got in on the opposite side, and Ken beside her.

The air-conditioned room felt cool and comfortable. Almost instantly, Ken began to feel the sweat drying on his body. But his leg — the one inside the plaster cast — began to itch like crazy, and the only thing he could do was to move the muscles in the leg to help relieve it.

A waitress came and began to hand them menus.

"Just coffee for me, Jean," Dottie told her.

"And a Coke for me," said Ken.

His sisters ordered Cokes, too.

The waitress scribbled down their orders, took the menus, and left.

Dottie wanted to know if they were returning from Candlewyck Speedway.

"In a way, yes," Ken replied, then explained what had happened there, and subsequently what had happened at the abandoned airport. She laughed over the episode about the two old men, then apologized, saying that it did sound funny to her.

Ken and the girls laughed, too. But he laughed less as he thought back to that scene — one old man shaking a finger at him while the other aimed his shotgun on the little red racer, threatening to "puncture it with holes." He could have been shot by one of those crazies.

The coffee and Cokes came, and the atmosphere calmed a little as Dottie looked seriously across the table at Ken and apologized for her bad behavior at her father's store the other day.

"Apologize? For what?" he said.

"Don't be naive," she told him. "You know what I'm talking about."

He did, but he thought he'd like to be subtle about it.

"I couldn't believe what Daddy had said about Scott," Dottie explained. "Later on, when he told me all about it, I was so angry I couldn't speak to anyone. I thought about calling you on the phone and apologizing to you, but I couldn't get myself to do it. I did plan on doing it sometime. I'm glad I saw you on the street," she added, smiling.

He grinned. "Me, too."

"You know, it was just two days before he stole that engine that he had asked Daddy to sponsor him? Doesn't that amaze you?"

"Sure it does. Scott must have had that robbery all planned, figuring he would never be suspected if he had your father sponsoring him."

"Right. And if your brother hadn't been near there at the right time he might still be driving with Daddy as his sponsor."

"My brother?" Ken frowned. "What's he got to do with it?"

Her eyes focused on him. "Dana's the one who saw Scott's pickup truck driving toward Daddy's automobile parts store that morning. Then he sneaked over to Scott's place and saw the engine in their garage. Didn't Dana, or Daddy, tell you that?"

He hesitated. "No," he answered finally, dumbfounded at the news. His hands trembled. He set the glass of Coke down and clenched his fists.

Dottie looked at him gravely. "Ken, I didn't mean to upset you."

He relaxed his fists. "Sorry." He forced a grin. "I guess I've been a little touchy since I broke my foot."

He put the glass to his lips and took a couple of swallows.

Ask Dusty Hill for it, Dana had said. *I'm sure he'll give it to you.* No wonder he was sure that Dusty would put up the bail money for him. He felt that Dusty owed him for having told him who had swiped his engine.

"How was Dana sure it was Scott who had stolen the engine?" Ken asked.

"He was coming home late from Nick's place that night and saw Scott's truck drive into the lane heading toward the rear of Wade Mall," Dottie

97

explained. "Only he didn't realize it was Scott's truck at the time. Scott had a sign on the side of it advertising Daddy's store. But he saw the first three letters on Scott's license plate."

"R stands for Rat," Ken said.

"Right. Rat, his nickname." She shook her head and looked away for a minute. "What an actor. He could be so charming! Ugh!" She turned back to him. "Anyway, when Dana found out that an engine was stolen from Daddy's store — "

"I told him," Ken cut in.

Her eyebrows raised. "Oh?"

"Go on," he said.

"Well, he sort of added two and two, drove up to Scott's place, and saw the engine in Scott's father's garage."

"And got away without being seen?" Ken shook his head, incredulous. "You know, that brother of mine has a lot of guts, too."

"But he *was* seen," said Dottie. "By Scott's father."

Ken and his sisters listened avidly to her as she went on to explain about the threat Mr. Taggart had made against Dana, and Dana's promise not to inform the police on them if Scott returned the engine to the store.

"Wonder why he promised that?" Ken muttered.

Dottie laughed. "Maybe to save his life," she said. "Scott's father had a shotgun on him."

"A shotgun?" Ken gulped. Then he winced as he visualized the scene in his mind and compared it with the experience he had had not too long ago with the two old men. Both he and Dana could look back sometime and thank their stars they hadn't been shot.

But, suddenly, Ken's mood changed. Dana had seemed so distant since Ken inherited the car; why the change now? Did Dana want to become better friends, or did he want something else? Ken couldn't help being suspicious.

He tried to hide his emotions as they talked a bit more. Then he glanced at his watch and saw that it was close to one o'clock.

"No wonder my stomach's been talking back to me," he said. "It's past lunchtime. I've got to get home."

"I'm glad we could get together for a minute, Ken," Dottie said, scooping up the check. She smiled. "This is on me."

"Okay. Thanks."

He thought about asking her to go to a movie

with him sometime, but decided he could call her on the telephone later in the week.

He slid out of the booth, picked up his crutches, and hobbled out of the place, his sisters flanking him like bodyguards.

In the truck the girls started to bring up the subject of Dana's connection with Scott Taggart's theft of the engine, but Ken cut them short. He said he didn't want to hear another word about it.

He didn't, but their mention of it aroused his suspicions again. Did Dana use his information about the engine to get Dusty to sponsor his brother? Ken tried to think of a way to tell Dana that it was fine for him to tell Dusty who had stolen the engine, but he didn't like the idea of Dana using it to *bribe* Dusty into sponsoring him.

Dana wasn't home when Ken and the girls got back. Their father, sitting on a high-backed rocking chair on the rear porch, said he had gone to work. "Well, did you have fun?" he wanted to know, turning his head slightly to gaze at the little red car on the trailer.

"No, Dad, I didn't," Ken said, and explained briefly the trouble he had had at Candlewyck, and with the two men at the abandoned airfield.

"Maybe it's just as well," his father murmured. He leaned forward and spat over the edge of the porch. "One of these days an ambulance will be driving you to a hospital again, and maybe the next time it'll be for something worse than your leg."

Ken smiled, and patted him on the shoulder. "I'll be all right, Dad. Don't worry."

He hobbled into the house, had a drink of ice-cold tea from the refrigerator, then sat down and tried to think of where else he could take the Chevy to run passes. He knew of several macadam roads some fifty or sixty miles south of Wade, where a contractor had started a development and had his plans go awry. But Ken discarded the idea, figuring it was too far to drive.

Dana pulled in on his Kawasaki at twenty after three. Ken heard the motorcycle as he stood in the living room, doing stretching exercises. He continued to do them for a few more minutes, quitting when he heard the kitchen door open and Dana come in.

He stood there in the room without his crutches, his stomach tightening as he waited for Dana. Soon Dana came into the room, holding his helmet under his arm. He smiled as he greeted Ken, then the smile faded as he saw the strange look on Ken's face.

"Hey, what's up?" he said. "You look upset."

"I *am* upset," Ken snapped. "I just found out why Dusty decided to sponsor me instead of Taggart."

Dana frowned. "Did he tell you?"

"No. Dottie told me about your part in recovering the engine, and I put two and two together. She thought I knew. Look, I agree it was real good of you to do what you did in finding out who had stolen Dusty's engine, but I want to know why you're so anxious all of a sudden for me to drive for Dusty. You haven't seemed to want to be friendly lately; so if this is some way to get your hands on Li'l Red, you — "

"Wait a minute, Ken. You — "

" — can just forget it!" Ken cut in sharply.

Dana stared at his brother. "Why, you little twerp! You think I'm so anxious to get my hands on that car? I wouldn't give you the satisfaction now of telling you why I asked Dusty to let you drive! But why don't *you* try to figure out the right answer, *brother?*" And Dana whirled and marched out of the room.

ELEVEN

DANA STORMED OUT of the house, leaving by the front door to avoid being seen by his father.

He put on his helmet, buckled it, and got on his motorcycle. He kicked the starter and took off, dirt bursting from the spinning rear tire and clattering up against the fender.

He tore down the street, breaking the speed limit by ten miles an hour for almost two blocks before he throttled back. But he still kept it a couple of miles over the legal speed limit.

Who in heck did Ken think he was by talking to him like that, anyway?

Then he thought, darn it, what's gone wrong with us? How can my own brother be so suspicious of me? Maybe I *was* jealous about the car, but I'd never do anything that would harm Ken!

He might as well have said he's disowned me. What's the sense of being a brother if you can't help out one another sometimes?

He drove block after block, not knowing or caring where he was going. Then he thought of Sally — Sally Biemen — and made a right-hand turn at the next intersection.

Sally was a six-foot, interesting-looking brunette he had met at a motorcycle slalom some eight months ago. She had her own bike, a 125cc Honda that she drove back and forth to work. Somehow they had gotten to like each other and had gone out a couple of times a month. She lived alone in a one-room apartment on Casey Street.

He arrived there shortly, left his bike in the driveway, and walked into the apartment building and up the stairs to the second floor. He knocked on her door, tap-tippy-taptap, a sound that had become their signal.

A few seconds later the door opened and she was there, staring at him, her blue eyes shining.

"Dana!" she said. "What a surprise!"

"Yeah, I imagine it is," he murmured. "Can I come in?"

"Of course, silly."

He entered and tossed his helmet on the couch.

Then he sat down and sprawled his long legs out in front of him.

She closed the door. "What happened? You look as if someone's put you through the wringer."

"You're right. My brother."

"Ken?"

"Yes. Ken. Got any beer?"

She didn't drink the stuff, but she kept a few cans of it in the refrigerator for the times when friends dropped by.

"There's some left. I'll get it for you."

"Never mind. I'll get it."

He rose, went to the refrigerator, and took out a can. He cracked it open, carried it back to the couch, and held it until Sally placed a coaster on the coffee table. He set the can on it and looked with disinterest at the moisture that was forming on it.

Sally sat down on an easy chair across from him. She was wearing a white blouse and blue slacks with tiny anchors down near the bottom of each pant leg. A Saint Christopher medal hung on a slim chain around her neck.

"Want to tell me about it?" she said.

"I don't know," he said. "I just had to get away,

and this is the best place I thought of getting away to."

She didn't press him. She just kept looking at him as if in hopes that if she looked long enough she could figure out why he needed to be there.

He liked that about her. She was no gabby-mouth, nor was she inquisitive.

She reached over to the coffee table, opened a silver-plated case that was on it, and took out a cigarette. Then she picked up a small, plastic replica of a Civil War cannon, flicked the back end of the barrel with a finger, and lit the cigarette with the flame that burst forth from the front end of it.

She took a drag on the cigarette, then handed it to him. He took it and automatically placed it between his lips.

"Would you like to stay for supper?" she asked quietly.

He shrugged. "You sure you want me to?"

"I wouldn't ask you if I didn't, would I?" she said.

He smiled, took a long drag on the cigarette, held the smoke in his mouth for a while, then blew it out. It hit the coffee table, then began a slow, lazy ascent toward the ceiling.

There was the sound of a car outside. Dana's

preoccupied mind caught a familiar, subtle *ping* in the sound of the motor, but he dismissed it.

He leaned over, picked up the can of beer, and took a slug of it. How many cans of beer had Ken drunk in his life? he thought. Not many, I bet. Heck, by the time I was sixteen . . .

Someone was coming up the stairs. Someone with crutches.

Ken, Dana thought. What the heck did he want?

There was a knock on the door.

"It's Ken," Dana said thickly.

"Ken?" Sally frowned as she rose to answer the door.

She opened it, then calmly greeted Ken and invited him in. Dana didn't bother to look around. He didn't glance up until Ken came within his line of vision.

Before Ken could open his mouth to speak, Dana snapped, "Who invited you here? Get out."

Ken stood there, his hands gripping the handles of the crutches. "Dana, I'd like to speak to you a minute."

"Why? You got more insults you want to hand me? No, thanks. Sally, show my brother —"

"Dana, you've got to listen to me," Ken interrupted. "I'll only be a minute."

Dana's eyes narrowed. "How'd you know I was here?"

He saw Ken glance at Sally and then realized that Ken didn't need a dozen guesses to figure it out. It was either Nick's pool parlor or Sally's apartment, and Ken had chosen the more likely place where he'd expect to find him.

"Okay, never mind. Speak your piece and get out."

Ken hesitated. There was an awkward moment as Sally excused herself and went into the kitchen.

The brothers faced each other.

"I came to apologize for what I said," Ken began. "I got to thinking about it after you left, and I began to see your side of it." He paused briefly, then went on. "I appreciate what you did for me. I guess I couldn't let your first feelings about the car be part of the past, and I'm sorry I was suspicious of you." He took a deep breath and let it out. "Well, that's all I've got to say." He turned and headed for the door.

Spellbound, Dana watched his brother open the door and leave. He didn't move until he heard the familiar sound of the pickup start up and take off.

Sally came back into the room and stood in front of the door, silent, her hands clasped tightly close to her chest.

Dana squashed out the cigarette on the ashtray and got up. He picked up his helmet. "Give me a rain check on that dinner, Sally. Okay? See you later."

He went to the door, opened it, and walked out.

TWELVE

IT WAS on a Wednesday two weeks later, and two days after the cast was removed from his leg, that Ken drove over to Dusty Hill's auto parts store and told Dusty he was in tip-top shape for Saturday afternoon's race and was anxious to run a few passes.

Dusty glanced at Ken's legs, first one and then the other, and broke into a wide smile. "I can see you're good as new," he said.

"There's a clinker in the works, though," Ken said, and explained about the moratorium placed against him at the Candlewyck Speedway.

"Moratorium?" Dusty echoed, his eyes turning yellow. "Who said so, and why?"

"Buck Morrison did. His first excuse was that I had a cast on my leg. When I told him I couldn't believe that, because the cast was on my left leg and I used my right to drive with, he told me the truth. Somebody called him up and told him that he and some other guy would not drive in a race if I was allowed on the track, because I'd been drinking before I had gotten into that accident."

Dusty's jaw muscles twitched. "Why didn't you tell me this before?" he asked.

"I wanted to wait till I had the cast off."

"Wish you hadn't." His eyes focused on Ken's. "Was that true? Did you drink before you got in that accident?"

"No. I have a beer now and then, but that's all," Ken answered evenly. "Anyway, that accident was caused by a bad brake cylinder which 'Rat' Taggart, himself, discovered for me." He went on to explain that it was at his brother Dana's suggestion that he had asked "Rat" to look at the car.

Dusty frowned. "Did you tell Buck that?"

"I couldn't," Ken replied. "He wouldn't listen to me."

Dusty nodded. "I see." He squinched his eyes as he looked at Ken again. "Got any ideas who called Morrison?"

Ken shrugged. "There is no one who would have a reason to lie about me except the same guy who looked at my car, 'Rat' Taggart."

"Right. His name was the first to pop into my mind, too. He's got lots of reasons for wanting you not to race, and, from what he's done to me, I'm sure one fat lie about you hasn't bothered his conscience one bit." He raised a finger. "Excuse me a minute."

He picked up the phone directory, found the number he wanted, then took the phone off its cradle and dialed.

"Hello. Buck? This is Dusty. How you doing?"

For a few seconds Dusty and Buck Morrison exchanged idle chatter, then Dusty got to the point and asked Buck if he still intended not to let Ken Oberlin trial-run his car, or race at the track. He listened awhile, angry expressions crossing his face, then asked Buck if it happened to be "Rat" Taggart who had telephoned him.

A few seconds passed. "Come on, Buck. The truth. It *was* 'Rat,' wasn't it?" Dusty prodded him.

A few more seconds passed. Then Dusty nodded. "Just what I thought, Buck. Well, 'Rat' lied. He doesn't want to see young Ken Oberlin race because I fired him as my driver and hired Ken. I have a valid reason for doing so, but I can't explain it to you. Anyway, Ken Oberlin didn't drink before his accident. What happened was, his brake cylinder blew. He said he had tried to tell you that but you were too busy to listen." He paused. "Well, what do you say? Does he run on your track or doesn't he?"

Dusty listened for a while again to what Buck Morrison was saying, then a smile came over his face, broadening by the second; and when he hung up it was obvious that he had won his point.

"He said you can start using the track tomorrow morning," Dusty said. "And if you want to enter the race on Saturday or Sunday you'd better sign an entry form and pay your fee as soon as you can. There are already about forty drivers signed up for both events. The Eliminator is on Saturday, the E.T.'s on Sunday. You're racing in the Eliminator, right?"

"Right," said Ken. "And I'll make sure to pay my entry fee. Thanks for talking to Morrison."

"My pleasure. And I'll reimburse you for the entry fee."

"Right, thanks." Ken headed for the door.

"Hey, you're walking like a new man, Ken," Dusty called after him.

"Feel new, too," Ken replied.

He was up early the next morning, had breakfast, then drove to the track. His sisters begged to go with him, but he said that today, and tomorrow, Friday, he preferred to go alone. He intended to spend most of the time at the track and didn't want them to hang around there all that time by themselves.

Their hurt looks expressed their disappointment, but he hoped they understood.

He was one of the first drivers at the track. He went up to the timing tower to sign the entry form and pay his fee and found both Buck Morrison and Jay Wells busy talking and joking with a couple of racing drivers.

Buck caught his eye almost instantly, but looked away and continued to talk and laugh with the men until Ken drew up closer to them and made his presence obvious.

Everyone seemed to stop talking at once and glanced around at him. Buck's smile looked as if it were pasted on as his eyes dropped to Ken's legs and a surprised look flashed into them.

"So you've got the weight off," he said. "How you doing?"

"Fine." Ken noticed that there was nothing in Buck's expression that hinted of Dusty's phone call to him. He took a twenty-dollar bill out of his wallet. "My entry fee for Saturday."

"Okay. We'll get you signed up in a minute.

Would you like us to start scoring you points? You'll need them to qualify for the national championships."

"Not at this time," Ken said.

"Okay. You'll have to sign a waiver. Step over here to my desk."

Ten minutes later Ken was back in the pits, driving the red Chevy off the trailer. He thought he detected a hiss in the engine, but it cleared up and he drove the car to the area just south of the entranceway to the track, hung around while the tech men inspected the car, then drove it back up around the timing tower. He got out and put on his firesuit, helmet, and gloves, then got back in. One of the three track crewmen waved him toward the number two lane next to a black Ford and he accelerated the Chevy till he had it in place.

A blue, white-trimmed Plymouth was in front of him. He recognized it even without reading the name written in bright red script across the back of it: "Snakeman" Wilkins. Next to the Plymouth was a green Chevy.

The Christmas tree was there some twenty feet ahead, its staging lights turned on. Ken watched the bulbs flash on one by one, then heard the deafening roar of the two cars as they bolted forward, twin exhausts belching smoke as their wide rear tires took a firm grip of the asphalt and whisked machines and drivers down the arrow-straight lanes. Seconds later a huge amber light flashed on at the right side of the lanes, indicating that "Snakeman" Wilkins had won, although the wins and losses meant nothing now and were not recorded.

"Okay," said one of the crewmen to Ken and the driver of the black Ford, and motioned them forward into staging position.

Ken drove ahead. When the front wheels touched the electric staging beam the yellow pre-staging light flashed on and Ken stopped the car. In a second the Ford was also ready.

Tension mounted in Ken as he watched for the staging lights to turn on. Suddenly they did and the skin on his arms prickled.

This was only a trial run, but it still meant that he had to get the best performance possible out of the little red machine. She was known to have been a winner in the 11.00 to 11.19 E. T. bracket (determined by the car crossing the finish line *first* in the 11.00 to 11.19 seconds elapsed-time class; crossing it *before* 11.00 seconds meant a loss), but that was when Uncle Louis sat behind her wheel — he knew her like a mother knows her baby. He had bought her off a used-car lot and had transformed her into one of the fastest cars Candlewyck and a lot of other speedways had ever seen.

But those wins had *also* had a lot to do with Uncle Louis's knowledge of the garish collection of colored lights that stood on the tall stem in front of him. That intuition, that feeling that made you know the split second when the green "go" light flashed on, made the big difference between whether you won or lost.

Uncle Louis had had it, and it had made him a winner.

Ken hoped he'd have it soon, too.

One by one, at half-second intervals, as he watched, the five amber lights popped on.

Then the green light flashed on and he stepped on the gas pedal as if it were a deadly snake. The car sprang forward like a cat, its front end almost lifting off the asphalt, its wide rear tires spinning and biting into the hard surface in a desperate effort to get away from that spot as fast as they could.

Ken glanced at the speedometer as the needle climbed up above the fifty mark to the sixties . . . the seventies . . . the eighties . . .

It was about 105 when he flashed past the 1320-foot mark.

"Ken Oberlin in Li'l Red, thirteen point thirty-eight and one hundred six point twenty-eight miles an hour," came the announcement from the public address system. "That isn't bad driving for young Ken Oberlin, who's only sixteen years old. Jack Wheeler in the Ford, fourteen point eleven and ninety-seven point eighty-nine miles an hour. Maybe you haven't been feeding those horses the right kind of hay, Jack."

Thirteen thirty-eight, one oh six point twenty-eight, Ken reflected, disappointed. If Uncle Louis could have heard that he'd turn over in his grave.

Fifteen minutes crawled by before his next pass came up. This time he cut the time down by twenty-nine hundredths of a second.

On his next run he hit the gas pedal too soon and red-lighted. On the next he did it again, and thought he'd better sit out the next two or three passes.

He drove to the pits, unbuckled his seat belt, and got out of the car. He unzipped the firesuit partway to let the fresh breeze cool his skin, then walked over to the concession stand and bought a can of ice-cold ginger ale. He popped it open, took a long swig of it, then stayed there till he had emptied it.

It was half an hour before he made his next run.

This time he started off okay, but his time was slower by ten-hundredths of a second than it was on the first run, and he thought he'd better quit and go home. He had had Li'l Red running faster than that before, and he knew he could have her performing better again.

He got out of his gear, put the car back on the trailer, and drove home, pondering his mistakes and how to correct them when he returned to the track tomorrow.

It rained during the night. The thunder woke him and his first thought was whether it would continue to rain throughout the morning. If it did, the trial runs would be called off.

He didn't need that. What he needed was to get as much practice as he could.

The rain stopped before daylight. At nine o'clock he called the timing tower to ask if the track was going to be open. Jay Wells, answering the phone, said that the track was a little wet, but if it didn't rain any more they would open it at noon.

Ken thanked him and breathed easier as he hung up the receiver.

There was another string of cars pulling into the speedway when he got there. By the time he was able to run a pass it was almost one o'clock. His initial run was timed at 12.02, 112.96 miles per hour, his best yet.

The performance lifted his confidence to a new high, and even Jay Wells, speaking over the P.A. system, congratulated him for a "good drive."

He did another run in the twelves. Then something popped under the hood on his third run, slowing down the car, and he almost burst a blood vessel.

"Oh, no!" he cried. "What now?"

THIRTEEN

KEN SHOVED THE CAR out of gear and stopped some fifty feet farther down the lane.

He heard the clicking sound of the cooling engine, smelled the rancid odor of oil, and for a moment he wondered if a gasket had blown.

He started up again, listened to the droning sound, and gradually the smell of the oil disappeared. He shoved the lever into first gear, touched the gas pedal, and felt no response.

He pressed down harder on the gas. Still no response. A flash of irritation shot through him and he struck the steering wheel hard with the palm of his hand. He was no expert on cars, a situation he had to change as time passed. But he knew the trouble he had now. The clutch was shot.

A feeling of desperation took hold of him as he looked at the small crowd of racing fans standing around the pit stops, most of whom were friends of the drivers. The others had just come to see the trials. Now their attention was diverted to him and his little red car, and he felt hot and embarrassed.

He heard the sound of a car, looked in his rearview mirror, and saw the speedway's brown station wagon drive up behind him. The driver got out, ran forward, and wanted to know what the trouble was. Ken told him.

"Sit still," the driver said. "I'll get in front of you, hitch up a rope, and pull you to the pits."

In less than ten minutes the little red Chevy was sitting next to the trailer in the pit stop, a sick piece of machinery that needed a top-notch doctor to get her back in running order.

Ken felt hopelessly stranded. There was nothing he could do but get Li'l Red on the trailer, haul her over to Dusty's garage, and just hope that Dusty would let Rooster put in a new clutch. There was no other way. If Dusty didn't go along with that, Ken was sunk. He could get a new clutch put in eventually, but when? It took money.

He looked up toward the timing tower that lay

against a backdrop of cotton-white clouds and thought of calling up Dusty to break the bad news to him. He hoped that Dusty'd have Rooster drive over with the pickup and winch and haul Li'l Red to the garage.

Someone's face was up there in the window, shadowy eyes peering down at him.

Ken looked away, his feet like lead weights, and started toward the building. Just then he heard running footsteps behind him and, as he turned, a voice said, "Hey! Need some help?"

"Dana!" he exclaimed, surprised at the sight of his brother. "What are *you* doing here?"

"Came to see you drive. What do you think?"

Ken smiled, perplexed. He still couldn't believe that Dana would ever go out of his way to see him drive the Chevy.

"What happened?" Dana asked again, peering through amber sunglasses.

Ken told him.

"Oh-oh. What were you going to do? Call Dusty?"

"Yes. What else?"

"Don't," said Dana. "He might start to lose faith in you and the car and drop you. As a matter of fact, he'll find out anyway about your car breaking. I saw Dottie in the stands."

Ken sighed. He turned slowly, let his gaze sweep over the grandstand seats on the west side of the field, and saw some fifty spectators sitting there.

"Never mind," Dana said. "She's hard to see, even in that small crowd. But she's there."

"I guess she's interested to see what Li'l Red can do," said Ken.

"Don't be modest, brother," Dana said, grinning. "She's here to see what *you* can do. Look, I know just the guy to fix this baby — if I can get him to break away. He might want to bring some parts and tools with him and will have to know what kind of car he's going to work on. Got a pencil and paper?"

"In the glove compartment," said Ken. "Just a second."

He found a pencil and pad and began to jot down certain features of the car that he felt would help Dana's friend — or whoever he was — to bring what he needed to fix the car.

He tore off the top sheet and handed it to Dana. Dana read it over quickly, then looked at Ken. "This should do it. Stick around. I'll be back in a few minutes."

He took off on a slow run, heading for the timing tower.

Ken remembered another time when Dana had gotten a friend of his, at his father's suggestion, to check out the brakes on the little red racer. But that friend — Scott "Rat" Taggart — was no friend anymore.

Who else did he know who could fix a clutch?

Dana was back in less than ten minutes, saying that he had gotten the guy and that the information Ken had written down for him seemed to be all that he needed to have in order to fix the damaged clutch, or put in a new one, depending.

"Who *is* this guy who's supposed to be such a genius?" Ken asked. "I thought Rooster, Dusty's mechanic, was the only car genius in town."

Dana smiled. "Phil Bettix, head mechanic at Troy's Garage. But he can't come so he's sending one of his better men, an Otto Dirkson." He frowned. "Be glad he's sending somebody. I wasn't sure he would."

"What do you mean?"

Dana pushed the sunglasses up slightly on the bridge of his nose. "I met him through Nick. Now don't worry," he went on quickly as Ken's eyes narrowed at the sound of Nick's name. "Phil's okay. He's got a mind of his own and he plays a mean game of pool. I know. I played him one night and he trimmed the pants off of me."

Ken didn't press him. He had no alternative now, anyway, but to go along with Dana.

About twenty minutes later a grimy white pickup truck pulled up behind the pit stop, came to a shuddering stop on the cracked asphalt, and a guy in a pair of oil-smeared coveralls hopped out of it.

He looked at the red car, then at Ken and Dana.

"That the car with the clutch trouble?"

"Right," Ken said.

The man nodded, then lifted a hydraulic jack off the back of the truck and immediately went to work jacking up the front end of the car. He lifted a creeper off his truck, set it on the asphalt, grabbed a handful of tools, then lay on his back on the creeper and rolled it under the car.

Ken looked at Dana. I wonder how long this is going to take? his eyes asked.

An hour and a half later Otto Dirkson, finished with the installation of a brand-new clutch, crawled out from underneath the car, released the jack, then got in the car and started it. He shifted the lever into the various gears and each time the car responded quickly and smoothly.

Without cracking the remotest smile he said, "There you are. Guaranteed to put you up front."

Ken smiled, pleased with his assurance.

"Tell Phil I'll square it with him," Dana said. He took a bill out of his pocket. "Here. This is for you."

Otto looked at the money, a ten spot. He started to reach for it, then withdrew his hand. "No, thanks. I — "

Dana pushed it into his hand. "Come on. Shyness will get you nowhere."

The mechanic took it, and the face that Ken thought didn't have a smile wrinkle in it, flashed a grateful grin.

"Thanks, mister," he said. Then he turned to Ken. "That's a new LK-ten clutch you've got in there, kid. It's got six clutch fingers made of forged steel, a cover made of ten-gauge steel, and a twelve-bolt pressure plate. It all spells great performance. I know. I put one in my sixty-eight sports car."

"Do you race it?" Ken asked.

"Used to, but now I'm just a Sunday driver."

Ken and Dana helped him reload the jack and his other equipment onto the pickup, then waved to him as he drove off.

"Take care, you hear?" he shouted back at them.

"Will do!" Ken answered. He turned and

looked at Dana. Their eyes met and for a moment an electric silence came between them. Ken wanted to say something. Just a thank-you seemed hardly adequate. But he didn't know what else to say.

He put out his hand and Dana took it. "Thanks, Dana."

"Don't thank me. Thank Otto." Dana laughed, then took his hand from Ken's and slapped him lightly on the shoulder. "Come on. Get in that little red baby of yours and show these jocks around here what you can do."

Ken watched his brother's back a minute as Dana walked away, suddenly realizing that he certainly owed him something now. Shaking his head, he approached the Chevy, got in, started it, and drove to the staging lanes.

Once again he was thrilled that Li'l Red was fixed and running — and within time to let him get in a few more passes.

He took his turn and blazed the tires down the 1320-foot lane, but he clocked in at only 14.59 seconds and 91.07 miles per hour.

It was a very disappointing run.

Heading back toward the staging lanes he tried to figure out what he'd done wrong. Had he favored the new clutch? Babied it because he was afraid it might blow, too?

He got back in line facing number two lane, knowing he had to do much better or kiss Saturday's race good-bye.

FOURTEEN

KEN RAN a couple of more passes, doing better each time by fractions of a second. He wasn't fully satisfied, but he decided to call it quits for today. He felt exhausted and ready for a good, cool shower.

He was about to drive the Chevy up on the trailer when he received a visitor.

"Hi," said a familiar voice.

"Dottie! Hi! I didn't think you enjoyed drags that much."

A light breeze fanned her hair. She was wearing a white T-shirt and blue jeans that hinted at her nice figure. "I love them," she said. "What happened to the Chev?"

"The clutch blew. Had a new one put in."

She frowned. "Who did the job? I know it wasn't Rooster."

"No. A mechanic who works for a friend of

Dana's did. I was going to call your dad but Dana thought I'd better not."

"Why? Afraid Dad might let you go?" Dottie said, hitting Dana's presumption right on the head.

Ken shrugged. "Dana was."

"And you?"

"I thought of it, but I had no other choice at the time. I was going to call your father when Dana showed up."

"Well, I can see where you and Dana might think that Daddy could possibly want to drop you, but I don't think he would," she said. She flashed a smile. "He likes you."

He laughed. Asking her if she liked him, too, was at the tip of his tongue. But he restrained himself, then drove the Chevy up on the trailer and secured it.

She came up to him and showed him a couple of theater tickets.

He stared at them and then at her. "What are those for?" he asked.

"Daddy bought them for tonight's play at Logan's Dinner Theater," she said cheerfully. "Something's come up and he can't make it. Would you care to go with me?"

"I'd love to. What's the show?"

"*The Sound of Music*. Have you seen it?"

"Never."

"Good. Can you pick me up at six-thirty?"

He thought a moment. "All I've got is this pickup and Li'l Red, you know," he told her. "And I just use Li'l Red for racing. Hey, I'll borrow my mom's Mustang."

Her eyebrows raised. "What's wrong with the pickup?"

He shrugged. "Nothing. I just thought — "

"That I might be too high class to ride in it to a dinner theater?" She laughed. "I get enough high class rides in that sports car of mine. A ride in a pickup will be a welcome change."

He grinned. "See you at six-thirty," he said.

He picked her up almost on the minute. They arrived early at the dinner theater, ate, then watched the play, which Dottie later confessed she had already seen four times.

After the show Ken drove her home. He couldn't think of when he had had a nicer evening.

He ran more passes on Saturday morning. His best clocking time was 11.87 seconds and 115.97 miles an hour. It qualified him easily for the afternoon's Eliminator race, but he doubted that such a time was fast enough to win it.

Nevertheless, that afternoon, in front of a jam-packed crowd of enthusiastic drag-strip fans, he won the first two runs — beating a Dodge and an Oldsmobile. The Olds had broken about a hundred feet from the starting line. Then he red-bulbed to a Camaro and came in third-round loser.

He could hardly sleep that night thinking about the loss. The red light was the bugaboo for all racers. Step on the gas a fraction of a second too soon and the devil would pop its big red eye.

On the following Saturday he was fourth-round loser, one round from being runner-up. His prize was a trophy and a check for five hundred dollars. Dusty shared Ken's jubilation over Ken's driving and the little red car's great performance.

"I knew you could do it, kid," Dusty praised him, perspiring as if he had driven the car himself. "One of these days you'll come out on top and it won't be long, either." He walked around the Chevy, examining its tires. "Take the car to the garage on Monday. I'll have Rooster groom it with four brand-new tires. These look pretty sick."

Ken showed him the five-hundred-dollar check he had won. "Here's my first big prize money, Mr. Hill. Shall we go to the bank so I can give you your forty percent?"

"Keep it," said Dusty, waving the check away.

"I'll start taking my share out of your next winnings."

Ken's respect and liking for the man who had gotten to trust him increased tenfold. "Thanks, Mr. Hill," he said cheerfully.

On Monday he trailered the Chevy to Dusty's garage and Rooster put on four new tires. Then he took the car to the speedway to begin another week of trial runs and saw a new competitor: someone he hadn't seen nor heard from since the theft of the engine from Dusty Hill's store. Scott "Rat" Taggart was driving a sky-blue Hemi Volare with his name emblazoned on all four fenders and another name painted in huge fire-red script on the sides. Ken looked twice to make sure he was seeing right: *Nick Evans*.

He never dreamed that Nick would ever sponsor a driver. But, somehow, he wasn't surprised that the driver he now sponsored turned out to be Scott "Rat" Taggart. Birds of a feather, he thought. He hated to think that Dana belonged to that clan. Maybe his brother would see the light someday and leave Nick Evans's company for good.

He ran a few passes before he and Taggart could no longer avoid getting within waving distance of each other. At first their eyes met and

Ken wondered whether Taggart would wave or speak to him. Without pausing too long he waved first. Taggart nodded in acknowledgment, then turned away.

A few minutes later Ken drove up to the staging lane for another trial run. Tensely watching the amber lights flash on, and anticipating the green, he jumped on the gas pedal too quickly and red-bulbed. Angry at himself, he was sure that Scott Taggart had seen him default and was probably snickering with pleasure.

Feeling hot and tense, he drove Li'l Red beyond the 1320-foot mark and headed for the pit stop. He was removing his helmet and firesuit when he saw Dusty coming toward him.

"How long have you been here, Mr. Hill?" Ken asked, surprised to see him. Dusty seldom left the store to watch the trials.

"About half an hour." Dusty jerked his head toward the lanes. "I see that 'Rat' Taggart's driving a Volare and that Nick Evans is sponsoring him."

"Yeah. And with Nick sponsoring him you can bet that there'll be a lot of money riding on him Saturday."

Dusty's eyes narrowed as he looked at Ken. "Scott worry you?"

"Not a bit."

"Good."

Smiling, Dusty left, headed for the parking lot. Ken watched him briefly, feeling a strong liking for the man. If only his father had the faith and trust in him that Mr. Hill did, he thought, much of his battle about racing cars, and growing up, would be won.

He finished removing his firesuit, then tossed all his gear into the pickup and drove home.

During the rest of the week he ran passes that put him solidly in the eleven-second category. Once on Friday he blazed down the quarter-mile strip in 10.48 seconds, clocking a speed of 117.09 miles an hour.

Although he knew that he was driving the little red Chevy at a pretty fast competitive clip, Ken figured that it was premature for him even to consider competing in the National Hot Rod Association's events. But it was something that didn't cost him a cent to dream about. Anyway, he knew he would have to finish school before he could start turning that dream into reality.

Drivers competing for championship titles earned points to qualify, but he wasn't interested in earning points just yet. He might think about that the first part of next year and start earning enough points to compete in a national event then.

The ultimate goal of the dedicated drag racer was to become the NHRA world champion, but to do so he had to win a certain number of national events, a certain number of divisional World Championship Series (WCS) races, *and* the World Finals — and do it during a nine-month racing season.

There were racers competing at the Candle-wyck Speedway on Saturday who were shooting for more points — this was permitted according to the regional rules — but it was up to the individual driver whether he wanted to earn points or not. Otherwise points were awarded automatically to the top drivers for top speed in their class, for low elapsed time, for establishing an official speed record, and for establishing an official elapsed-time record.

Aside from the points, there were prizes and trophies given to the winner and the first two runners-up on Saturday afternoons, which made the race worthwhile for any driver. Five thousand dollars went to the winner, twenty-five hundred to the first runner-up, and seven hundred and fifty to the second runner-up.

Minutes before Ken was going to leave for the

speedway on Saturday the phone rang. He was sitting on a lounge chair in the living room, discussing the upcoming race with Dana. His mother and the girls were on the sofa, preoccupied with costumes they were making for the church bazaar.

"Answer it, Janet," her mother said.

Janet laid down the costume she was working on and went to the phone. She spoke briefly into it, then held it away from her. "Dana, it's for you," she said.

Ken watched his brother as he got off the chair and went to the phone. Something seemed to have been on Dana's mind all the time he had been sitting there, Ken had noticed. He and Dana had talked, but at moments Dana seemed to have had his mind elsewhere. Did this phone call have anything to do with what he was thinking about?

Dana spoke into the phone for only a few seconds, then hung it up, a puzzled expression coming over his face. He smiled at his family, a smile that wasn't really genuine, Ken thought. "I've got to leave for a while," he said. "Be back later."

He went to his room, came out with his helmet, and left.

"Who do you suppose that was?" Mrs. Oberlin said.

"It was a man's voice," Janet said, picking up

the costume she was working on and settling herself back on the sofa.

Ken rose from the lounge chair, stepped into the dining room, then to a window facing the garage. He saw Dana put on his helmet, get on his motorcycle, and drive off. He didn't seem to be in a hurry, yet Ken felt that whoever had called him wanted to see him right away.

FIFTEEN

DANA BREEZED through the streets at a moderate clip, thinking about the brief telephone call from Nick Evans.

"This is Nick. I'd like to see you right away."

That was it. He had hung up without giving Dana a chance to say whether he could make it or not.

But that was Nick — blunt, abrupt, arrogant, and sure. He seemed to have no doubt that Dana could make it.

A heaviness settled in Dana's chest as he guessed Nick's purpose for calling him. Nick had given him a job to do. He wanted to know if it was done.

But he could have asked me that over the phone, Dana told himself. Why hadn't he?

Maybe Nick wanted to see him about something else.

He arrived at Nick's pool parlor, parked in the lot close to the entrance door, and went in, carrying his helmet under his arm.

Business was thriving. There were players at each table and customers waiting for their turns.

Nick, wearing a dark blue shirt with a white collar, was sitting on the stool behind the cash register, one leg cocked up against the counter.

"Hi, Nick," Dana greeted him. "What's up?"

Nick dropped the leg and folded his arms across his chest. A slow smile came over his mouth that put Dana instantly on guard.

"Did you do it?"

Dana stared at him. "No, I didn't," he said.

The smile vanished from Nick's mouth. "Why not?"

Dana cleared his throat. He took a glance at the customers, then looked again at Nick. "He's my brother, Nick," he said. "That's why."

"Oh. So now you've got a change of heart. He's your brother." The smile came back for just a moment. "Not too long ago you told me he was just like anybody else to you."

"That's changed."

"I see." Nick tapped his fingers against his bare arms. "You should have, Dana," he said without looking Dana in the eye. "You should have done like I told you. It would've been very easy for you to have done something to the carburetor, or the gas line, or even the clutch. Phil told me he had one of his men put a new clutch in Ken's car last week."

"Right," Dana said. "I was the one who called Phil."

"I know." Nick shook his head. "I put a lot of money on Taggart, Dana. A lot of money. But if your brother wins —" His voice trailed off and he shrugged.

"Sorry, Nick," Dana said. "I gave it a lot of thought. I just couldn't do it."

He turned and started for the exit door.

"Dana, just a minute."

Dana paused. He stood while Nick approached another door and opened it. Two guys rose from a table where they were playing cards and came swaggering out of the room. One was tall and had a deep dimple in his chin. The other was squatty, moon-faced, and wore a mustache.

Dana stared at them, knowing from their impassive expressions that Nick had other intentions in mind than to introduce them.

"These guys would like to see you in there, Dana," Nick said.

Before he knew what was going on, the two guys grabbed his arms and yanked him into the room. The door slammed shut behind them.

Dana was suddenly aware that something unpleasant was going to happen to him unless he acted first. He slugged the tall one on the head with his helmet, and swung the helmet back in time to strike the squatty one on the arm as the guy was about to hit him. Then Dana dropped the helmet and began to use his fists. He unleashed a a couple of hard rights to squatty's face, drawing blood as the second jab struck the man's nose.

A blow on the left side of his neck from the tall guy jarred him for a moment, but he turned and belted him a series of undercuts that sent Nick's thug crashing to the floor. Almost at the same time that the man was going down, the second man rammed into Dana with his mile-wide shoulders and drove him up against the wall. Dana, pinned there for a moment, turned so that he faced his opponent, dodged a blow directed at his jaw, then jerked up his right knee with all the power he could muster and jammed it against the man's face. A painful grunt tore from the guy as his head flew up and more blood spurted from his nose. He fell back, covering his face with his hands, and stumbled to the table where he sat down heavily, taking a handkerchief from his pocket to blot his bleeding nose.

Dana started to swing at the tall guy again but held up when he saw the man raise his hands in surrender.

"Hold it, buddy," the man pleaded, a bruise over his right eye turning black and blue. "Nick underestimated you. I don't think he knew you were a fighter."

"I only fight well against punks like you," Dana said, rubbing his knuckles.

He picked up his helmet and walked out, winking at Nick, who stood outside the door staring at him.

"See you at the track," Dana said, and left.

SIXTEEN

IT WAS LATE AUGUST and the rainy season, but the sky was clear and there was just enough breeze in the air to stir the trees surrounding the speedway.

Ken tried not to show his nervousness as he pulled on his firesuit, aware that he was the focus of attention of at least a half-dozen fans who had come to see him race. Dana and Dusty were in the pit with him, and somewhere up there in the crowded stands was the rest of his family.

His father hadn't wanted to come. It was only because his mother had said that school was starting soon and this was probably Ken's last race of the season that he had changed his mind.

Ken hadn't told anyone that this might be his last race. He saw no reason why he could not run passes a day or two each week after school and race occasionally on weekends. But he said nothing about this to his parents. He wanted to make sure his father came to see this race.

He saw Scott Taggart in the pits with a long-haired guy he didn't recognize and figured that Nick Evans must be somewhere nearby, too. Probably in the stands.

It would be something, he thought, if he and Scott had to pair off in one of the rounds. So far he hadn't learned how fast Scott's Volare was able to go.

There was a roar from the crowd as an announcement came over the public address system and the first of the sixteen pairings got under way. There were thirty-two cars entered. Each pairing and position had been decided beforehand according to the car's best qualifying time, and Ken's turn to run was sixth. The winners of the first two runs then paired off to race in the second round, the winners of the third and fourth runs paired off to race in the second round, and so on. The same system prevailed for the third, fourth, and fifth rounds. The winner of the fifth round was declared the winner and champion.

Ken watched the cars, both Fords, start with their front ends almost leaping off the asphalt, then settling to blaze down the lanes with smoke tearing from their rear tires.

They seemed to be even as they zoomed past the finish mark. Then, seconds later, came the announcement: "Winner of the first run, Jake Moller, at twelve point ninety-nine seconds and one hundred and ten point sixty-two miles an hour; Loser is Steve Blaser at thirteen point oh three seconds and a hundred and nine point ninety-nine miles an hour! Congratulations, Jake! Better luck next time, Steve!"

Again the crowd roared.

"Taggart must've been racing somewhere this summer," Dusty said, peering through gold-rimmed sunglasses. "Any scuttlebutt on him, Dana?"

"Yeah. He's been racing around the Palm Beach and Orlando area," Dana replied. "Did pretty well, too, I heard."

"He must have, or I don't think Evans would even consider having his name on Taggart's car. I wonder if it *is* his."

"It is," said Dana. "He bought it cheap, installed a new engine in it, and fixed it up into a good racer."

"New engine?" Dusty laughed. "I guess that

was his idea when he took that engine out of my store."

Dana smiled, then shot a sidelong glance at Ken. "Know what? I'd like to see you and 'Rat' Taggart match up with each other."

"You never know," murmured Ken.

He saw a deep, concentrated look come into his brother's eyes and knew that he was thinking of the trouble Taggart had caused them, trouble that finally had brought them closer together than they had ever been before.

The eliminations continued, losers falling by the wayside, winners coming back to meet the challengers in the next round.

The sixth run was ready to start. Dusty shook Ken's hand and wished him well. Dana waited till he got into the Chevy, his seat belt buckled and his helmet on.

"Good luck, brother," he said then, and shook his hand — a tight, warm squeeze.

Ken sat, tensed, waiting for the announcement from the timing tower. It soon came and he started the car.

"Ken Oberlin, number two staging lane, please," came Buck Morrison's voice. "Jim 'Little Beaver' Applejack, lane one."

Ken drove the Chevy up to the staging lane and

saw that the car he was driving against was a white 1974 Mustang with Jim "Little Beaver" Applejack's name splashed garishly across the side door and rear fender. Names of his sponsors were painted conspicuously over other parts of the car's body.

Ken eased the car up the asphalt till the Christmas tree lights flashed on, indicating he was properly staged. Then the Mustang moved up into position and seconds later the five amber lights on the tree began to flash on at half-second intervals.

The suit was becoming a sweatbox as Ken sat there, tense as a spring ready to uncoil. His foot was on the gas pedal, his left hand on the steering wheel, his right hand on the shifting lever.

He reminded himself of the two things he could do that would prove fatal: stepping on the gas pedal too soon or waiting a split second too long.

...Three...four...five...

Now! He jammed the gas pedal to the floor, and the car bolted like a Brahma bull, rear tires grabbing the asphalt like a million angry, hungry fingers.

Ken held the steering wheel in a firm grip, guiding the car down the quarter-mile strip at a speed that increased with each progressive millisecond.

"Come on, baby. Come on," Ken coaxed the blazing Chevy.

He had a terrible urge to look beside him to see where the other car was, ahead or behind. But he didn't dare. He wanted every bit of his attention riveted on the lane in front of him.

Seconds later he zipped past the finish mark and took his foot off the pedal. Glancing at the rearview mirror he saw that the bright light had turned on — on his side of the track! He had won!

His heart beating wildly, he slowed the car down and headed back toward the pits, his body bathed in sweat, as he waited for the speed and time announcements of the race.

Silence fell over the track as the announcer's voice crackled over the P. A. speakers: "Ladies and gentlemen, Ken Oberlin's time: eleven point thirty-four seconds and a hundred eleven point twenty-eight miles an hour. Jim 'Little Beaver' Applejack's time: twelve point thirty-two seconds and a hundred and nine point ninety-seven miles an hour. The winner — Ken Oberlin!"

A thunderous cheer broke from the crowd, while Ken's heart sang.

Dana came over to him and shook his hand again, a broad smile on his perspiring face. "Congratulations, brother. You ate up that track like a real pro."

"Thanks, Dana."

He looked around for Dusty Hill, and Dana told him that Dusty wanted to sit with Dottie during that round.

"I guess he felt he should be with her while you ran that race," Dana said. "It was a pretty important one."

An understatement, Ken thought. If he had lost it he'd be out of the competition. Now he had won the chance to compete in the next round.

He and Dana checked over the plugs, the carburetor, the gas lines, and the tires, and found everything to their satisfaction. When they finished they were standing close to each other. For a moment neither one of them said a word, as if each were trying to think of what the other was thinking.

Ken could hardly believe that Dana had made such an about-face in his attitude toward him. It was something he had hoped might happen, but he had never dreamed that it would.

A lump was in his throat as he said, "Know what, brother? I'm glad you're here."

"So am I," said Dana.

Finally the second round started. Ken won again and would now race in the third round. His time and speed were slightly slower than his run against Applejack, but they were still fast enough for him to beat out a Ford driven by "Battlescar" Jones.

"You see who's still running, don't you?" Dana said, looking down the line.

Ken followed his gaze, although he was sure he knew whom Dana was referring to. He had Scott "Rat" Taggart in the back of his mind all along. Taggart had been burning up the lanes at speeds in the 117-miles-per-hour range, beating his opponents easily, and chances looked good that the race was going to wind up with Ken and Taggart and last year's Division Champion, "Ace" Moreno, fighting for first place. In some quarters "Ace" was favored to win the race, but the way Ken and Taggart were blitzing their opponents, all three drivers were strong contenders.

It was ironic, Ken thought, that the race might end up that way. Although he felt sure that there was no hate between him and Taggart, he was sure that Taggart had no love for Dana.

Because of Scott's feelings toward Dana, Ken had no doubt in his mind that Scott was going to try his best to beat Ken if the final round was between them. He knew there were two important values at stake for Scott Taggart: the humiliation over the theft, and the name of Nick Evans as his sponsor — Nick, who was known to bet heavily on cards, horses, and cars.

Ken won the third round in the first one hundred yards when the Chevy he was racing against broke. He later found out that a stripped fuel line had caused a massive fuel leak in the car.

The cleanup crew hurried out onto the lane with soap and water and scrubbed it clean in minutes.

The fourth round came up and Ken saw that he was paired with a Camaro driven by Al "Grease" Adams, another driver the racing brotherhood had learned to respect.

They drove up to the staging lanes, gave the thumbs-up sign to each other, then turned their full attention to the Christmas tree. The winner of this round faced the winner of the round between Scott Taggart and "Ace" Moreno for the first prize of five thousand dollars and the Pro Stock Eliminator Trophy.

The lights began to flash, then the last of the five amber lights popped on and Ken pressed his foot on the gas pedal. The little Chevy leaped forward, tearing down the lane like a red streak, front wheels almost rising off the asphalt, rear tires spinning, smoke streaming in gusts behind it. The cars were running hub to hub as they sprinted down the lane, though Ken feared the Camaro was just slightly ahead of him.

Then, seconds later, both cars zipped past the 1320-foot mark and Ken saw, in the rearview mirror, the bright light flash on, again on his side of the track! He had won!

With hammering heart, he drove back to the pits to listen for the timer's announcement. He hopped out of the car, took off his helmet, and heard Buck Morrison's voice boom over the public address system. "Ladies and gentlemen, the time for Al 'Grease' Adams's run: eleven point sixty-one seconds and one hundred sixteen point forty-eight miles per hour!"

A roar exploded from the crowd, then diminished again to silence. Breathless, Ken waited for the voice to continue.

"The time for Ken Oberlin's run: eleven point thirty-two seconds and one hundred sixteen point ninety-four miles per hour. The winner — Ken Oberlin!"

The roar exploded again, this time louder and longer than the time before. Ken lifted his arms in a wave to the fans, then had to get back into his car to sit down and relax. Realizing that he had won the run that was going to put him into contention for first place was almost more than he could bear.

Dana's perspiring face glistened as he smiled and stretched his hand out to Ken. "You did it again, brother. One more to go."

One more, thought Ken, the pulse throbbing in his temples. With whom was it going to be? "Rat" Taggart or "Ace" Moreno?

He took off his firesuit and stood in his short-sleeved shirt and cut-off pants, listening to the crowd cheer as Taggart's name was announced as a driver in the first runner-up race. But, as "Ace" Moreno's name was announced, the applause was overwhelming. There was no doubt in Ken's mind who their favorite driver was.

The race began, both drivers starting off superbly. Then, seconds later, it was over, and what seemed like a deafening quiet hovered over the fans as the light flashed on down the track for the winner. Then the silence broke and a smattering of cheers and applause went up for Taggart, the winner over Moreno. It was obvious the fans were disappointed.

Taggart's time: 11.10 seconds and 117.59 miles per hour.

It was the best recorded time so far today.

Ken wished he had time to take a shower to wash off the sweat, cool his hot body, and relieve the tension that waiting for this important moment had built up in him. But all he could do was stand there and try his best to ignore the sticky humid air that was thick enough to slice with a knife.

"Well, Ken, it's down to the wire," Dana said. "You and Taggart. I hope you'll show him your tail when you shoot down that lane."

"Me, too," Ken replied.

Several minutes later a call came from the timing tower for the two finalists to start their cars and drive up to the staging lanes.

"Good luck, brother," Dana said, shaking Ken's hand.

Ken thanked him.

There was strength in Dana's grip, and Ken felt a tightness in his chest as he looked into his brother's eyes. He didn't have to wonder how Dana felt now that he, Ken, had gotten this far in the race. Seeing the proud gleam in Dana's eyes told him all he needed to know.

He got into his firesuit and then into the car. He put on his helmet and gloves, then started the car and headed for the staging lanes.

"Scott 'Rat' Taggart, number one lane, please. Ken Oberlin, number two," came the announcement from the timing tower.

Taggart got to the lane first. Two seconds later Ken drove up to his. As they sat in their cars side by side, Taggart glanced at Ken, his eyes like blue ice behind the plastic shield. Ken nodded to him, and Taggart raised a thumb in acknowledgment.

A crewman motioned them to approach the staging beams. Ken edged the Chevy forward till the staging light on the Christmas tree flashed on. Scott Taggart echoed the move with his Volare. In a moment both cars were aligned.

Suddenly the staging lights flashed on, then the ambers. The countdown started. One ... two ... three ...

Ken's mouth was cotton-dry as he watched the lights flick on. His body was like wound steel as he concentrated one hundred percent on the lights. Right now nothing else mattered.

He saw the fifth light flash on. Then, almost instinctively, he jammed his foot on the gas pedal as the green light flashed on. The front end of the car leaped up slightly, then came down, and for an instant panic shot through Ken as he thought that he might have started too soon.

But the red foul light had not gone on: he was all right.

The red Chevy roared down the lane, smoke blazing from the rear tires as they bit, chewed, and ripped at the asphalt.

Ken kept his gaze away from the speedometer. He didn't want to know how fast Li'l Red was going. She was going as fast as she could.

He was about two-thirds of the way down the lane when suddenly, from the corner of his eye, he caught a glimpse of Taggart's car veering off the lane toward him. He almost froze as the Volare rammed into the left side of his Chevy and shoved it off the lane. Gripping the wheel firmly so he wouldn't lose control of the car and probably strike the guardrail, risking a serious accident, Ken quickly took his foot off the gas pedal and let the car roll to a gradual stop on the grass.

Anger swept in a tidal wave through him. *Taggart, I could kill you!* his mind screamed.

He glanced over at the Volare and saw that Taggart was back on his lane, but had slowed the car down and was peering at him through the side window. Because of the shield of Taggart's helmet

Ken wasn't able to clearly see the expression in his eyes or on his face.

Dana came sprinting from the pits. He hopped over the guardrail, rushed to the Chevy, and flung open the door on Ken's side.

"You all right?" he gasped, his face chalk-white with worry.

"Yeah, I'm okay."

Dana glanced over his shoulder at the Volare. " 'Rat' Taggart," he said, bristling with anger. "The name is too good for him."

He turned back to Ken. "He rammed into you deliberately, you know that? He saw you were winning so he did what he felt he had to do — ram into you and hope that the judges will say it was an accident and demand another race."

"Maybe. Maybe not," said Ken.

"Look," Dana said, peering hard at him, "I know for a fact that Nick's got a pile of money on him. I never told you this, but Nick wanted me to do something to your car that would've stopped you in the first round. I wouldn't do it. I couldn't, I told him. Not to my own brother. Not to *anybody*." He paused. "I had to bust a couple of faces when I told him I wouldn't."

Ken stared at him. "Hey," he said, grinning, "maybe we'll become real close friends after all."

Dana put a hand on his shoulder and squeezed it. "Why not?"

Some minutes later an announcement came from the timing tower. "Attention, ladies and gentlemen," said Buck Morrison's voice. "My partner, Jay Wells, and I, as the event directors, along with the technical committee, have discussed the last round just run between Scott 'Rat' Taggart in lane number one and Ken Oberlin in lane number two, and we have come to a decision. We had videotaped the race and ran it over a couple of times here in the timing tower to make certain that our decision is fair, honest, and conclusive.

"We have decided unanimously that crossing the strip's center line, and the outer extremity line as noted in the rule book, was a deliberate move on Scott 'Rat' Taggart's part, and therefore an infraction. Based on that decision the winner of the final race, the five-thousand-dollar prize, and the championship is — Ken Oberlin!"

Ken listened to the words in stunned silence.

"You won it, brother!" Dana cried, pulling him out of the car and throwing his arms around him. "You won it!"

Ken still felt in a state of shock as, seconds later, Dusty Hill and Dottie came rushing toward him

160

and threw their arms around him, too. Then his mother, father, and sisters were surrounding him and showering him with praise, congratulations, and kisses.

For a long moment he met and held onto his father's gaze.

Then a smile came over his father's raw-boned face and he said, "Son, I wish that your Uncle Louis could be here to see you. I'm sure he would be very proud of you. Just like I am."

Ken felt a tightening in his throat. "That last thing you said, Dad," he murmured. "That's what I wanted to hear."

Then he put his arms around his father again, squeezed him tightly, and felt his father's arms squeeze him in return.